# AT THE GATE

## TREY STONE

Inked in Gray Press

www.inkedingray.com



ISBN 978-1-952969-07-2 (ebook) |978-1-952969-06-5 (print)

Cover design and art by Matt Barnes

*This book is dedicated to Maria, who was awarded her Ph.D. while I was writing this book. She waited three hours to tell me because I had told her "I didn't want to be disturbed."*

*I aspire to be as great as you one day.*

I don't want to be misleading by claiming that all the experiences in this story are mine alone, but they are all things that I've lived through or experienced through others.

This piece of fiction seeks to explore how those feelings manifested within me at the time.

Pain is pain, regardless of the shape it takes.

I don't want to promise that you'll find a way out of any struggles you might be dealing with, through this book. But I hope that maybe you can find understanding, or even solace.

- Trey

J oseph rang the bell for the fifth time. The loud, dreadful chime echoed throughout the sparsely decorated lobby. The room had a reception desk on one side, a doorway to a dining lounge directly opposite, and a big old stairwell at the end.

"Hello?" he called into the dark room behind the desk. It was eerily quiet in the hotel, but he thought he heard people moving around in that back room: shuffling around, feet dragging across the moldy carpet as if they'd heard him come in but couldn't be bothered to get up.

Turning in a half-circle, Joseph wondered if he was even at the right place. It didn't look like there was anyone in the lobby. It was so quiet, so empty. But when Joseph had mentioned *The Gate,* the driver who brought him there hadn't even questioned him. This had to be it.

*This is the place where I'll end it all. It's perfect.*

"Hello, is there anyone—"

"Yes?" a hard voice asked from behind him.

Joseph startled and smashed his hip into the side of the reception desk with a painful groan. "Holy hell, you scared me. Do you work here?"

"Of course I do."

The man—or boy, rather—looked too young to work there. His clothes were too big for his arms, his shirt too long at the sleeves, his jacket too wide across the shoulders. He had thin, black hair that fell into his eyes.

"Hi, I've booked a room. Joseph P—"

"Of course, Mr. Podwall. We've been expecting you."

When the boy spoke his name, Joseph's stomach sank. The way he said it, with familiar melancholy—or was it disdain?—made Joseph uneasy.

"Good, you got my booking then, I wasn't sure if—"

"Frank told us. Like I said, we've been expecting you."

"Frank? The driver?" *Wasn't that what the cab driver had said his name was?*

Joseph couldn't quite remember, and he didn't recall giving the driver his own.

"Sure, why not," the boy behind the desk said. He turned a few pages in a large book, making an entry here and there.

Joseph heard movement behind the boy again, in the office —or whatever the hell it was—and leaned over to see a figure glide past on the dirty, red carpet. Must have been who the boy was referring to when he said 'us.'

"There you go, Mr. Podwall. Welcome to The Gate." The boy handed him a metal key. It was large and cold, ornate like the rest of the hotel. It felt heavy in Joseph's hand.

"You're in room 704. Top floor. The elevator isn't in working order I'm afraid." The boy smiled a far too toothy smile, giggling as he did so.

Joseph didn't get the joke and wasn't about to ask what was so funny.

"Leave your luggage here. I'll have someone bring it up to your room."

"It's not that heavy. I can grab it myself," Joseph said as he reached for his suitcase, but with a sharp movement, the boy cut his hand in front of him as if to say *Stop!*

"Leave it, Joe!"

He left his luggage where it was, slowly drawing his hand back to his side. Joseph might have been scared if he wasn't so confused by the boy's behavior.

The boy's face brightened, but it was too forced to be genuine. Like a cheap Halloween mask, one of those rubber ones, trying to fit over a face that was too small.

"Sure, I'll leave it here then," Joseph said after a moment. "And don't call me Joe."

He had always hated being called Joe ever since he was little. He was Joseph Podwall, and he was to be a proper little boy.

Joseph turned around and saw stairs next to the elevator at the end of the large reception. They snaked their way up, spiraling along, wrapping around elevator. It didn't look like the elevator was out of business—no sign or barrier across the gate—but Joseph wasn't going to turn around and argue with the young receptionist, so he started up the stairs.

*It's not like I plan on staying long anyway.*

The stairwell was dim and heavy, only a few small lights spaced far apart. The same weirdly-patterned red carpet stretched between the walls, which were decorated with dirty-yellow wallpaper until halfway up the wall where it became ocean green. The wallpaper peeled off at the top, below the delicately-carved crown molding. Their fragile appearance made it seem like the walls would collapse in on him as he made his way up.

Joseph stopped in front of the elevator on the next landing, out of breath. Age had caught up with him and his balding head—which hadn't had more than a handful of hairs since his early twenties—and now he needed a moment. His thighs burned, and his knees ached.

*I don't regret leaving my luggage behind.*

There was a door to the hallway in front of him, slightly

ajar, and he could see that the next door behind it read *301. Am I really only on the third floor? I walked up five or six sets of stairs already.*

Inside the hallway, he saw someone whisk past the door to 301. Joseph swore it was the same person he'd seen in the room behind the reception downstairs. Same stature, same gait. But then again, he hadn't really gotten a good look at them.

After a deep breath, he followed the winding steps around the elevator, continuing upward. To take his mind off the laborious ascent, he looked down at the key in his hand, noticing it didn't have a tag. Not even a piece of string. It was simply a big, old, iron key.

*Bit unprofessional. What if I forget on my way up? I'd have to go back downstairs just to ask them again. The receptionist said 704, didn't he?*

Joseph drew heavy gulps of air. Even thinking too much exhausted him more.

On the fifth floor, the ceiling became lower, the carpet was darker. Everything seemed a bit smaller, as if the walls were leaning in.

The key dropped from his hands. *Why didn't I put it in my pocket?* He was sweating so much as he made his way up the stairs that it had grown slippery in his hands. But the bigger problem was that he couldn't see where the key had gone. He turned in circles where he stood. *It can't have gotten far. It has to be around here somewhere.*

"Looking for this?" A man stood in the doorway between the stairwell and the rooms on the fifth floor, a large metal key in his shaking hand. He was old—very old—his hair and beard were pale white, and he looked ready to collapse at any second from the sheer weight of a long-lived life on his shoulders.

"Thank you, but I don't think that's mine," Joseph said

carefully. "I had barely rounded the steps here, there's no way that can be my—"

"Room 704?" the man asked, shuffling over. He walked with a heavy limp, his hand shaking even more as he handed the key to Joseph.

"How did you know?"

"Got to be more careful, Joe," the man said, pointing to the number on the key. Right there at the base were three large numbers engraved in the metal.

704. *How did I miss that?* Joseph looked up at the man hesitantly, slowly accepting the key. "How did you know my name?"

"I overheard you talking to Bryan downstairs, I did, as you checked in. Didn't mean to pry, no, nothing of the sort. Difficult to keep to yourself in here, at The Gate." He turned, leaving Joseph at the bottom of the stairs leading to the sixth floor.

Joseph tried to figure out if what the man was saying was true. Sure, the old man could have overheard the boy in the reception, but how did he get up here so fast?

"What's your name?" Joseph called, but the man was gone.A loud whirring noise from the walls in the middle of the stairs startled him.

*Elevator is out of business, huh?* That probably explained how the man had gotten there. Joseph shook his head, turning to carry on up the stairs.

When Joseph arrived on the seventh floor, he realized it wasn't an illusion. The hotel *was* getting smaller. The stairwell, which could easily accommodate three people side by side at the bottom, barely had enough room for him to walk through. The doorway leading to the rooms was so low that Joseph had to hunch over, even though he wasn't a particularly tall man.

He looked left and right to see if there were any indications of where 704 might be, but saw no signs, no plaques, no detailed floor map. It couldn't be far away, it was only the fourth room on the floor. *Which way do I go?*

The hallway to the left snaked right at the end, but looking to the right, he saw that it curved right as well. *That's weird. It looks like the hallways don't meet up. Or am I thinking about this all wrong?*

He ended up going right, following the hallway as it turned. Joseph couldn't help but think that if it kept turning, it would eventually take him right back to the stairwell somehow.

As Joseph passed room 701, he was happy to see he was on the right track and wasn't going in the wrong direction. But room 702 never appeared.

There was a door marked *Private* and then one labeled *Supplies,* and then he came to room 703.

*Must have passed 702, I suppose.*

Unexpectedly, there were steps. Two up, then another. The hallway curved briefly right, then suddenly took a hard left. Joseph had never been so disoriented in his life, and he spent a lot of his time in old hotels.

The next plaque read 705.

"Wait, what?" he blurted, turning around to look back down the hallway. He hadn't passed any doors since the steps. How could he have passed 704?

Farther down the hall, he caught sight of someone disappearing into a room.

"Excuse me?" he called, but they didn't hear him—or didn't care—because they ignored his call and locked the door behind them.

He ran up to their room and saw 708. *What the hell?*

He started walking back down the winding hallway. He couldn't remember it curving like this. Now the ceiling was angled above him. How could he have not noticed that.

He took the two steps up . . . Hadn't the steps been going up when he came this way earlier? Shouldn't they go down instead?

Then out of the blue, there it was: 704. *How did I miss this?*

He turned from side to side. This was the only room on either side of the hallway—in fact, it was the *only* door. *Was I that caught up in my own thoughts?*

His heart pounded in his chest as he studied the door in front of him. *I—Oh, I can't even be bothered thinking about it. Old buildings do this, don't they?*

He placed a sweaty hand against the wood of the door. *But this is it. The place I came here for. My last room.*

Sliding the key into the lock, Joseph was relieved to learn that he indeed had the right key and the right room. The door unlocked straight away, and though it was heavy, it swung open without issue.

It was the smallest hotel room he'd ever seen. The ceiling was angled, lower on the left where the door swung in. A huge gash in the ceiling told him previous guests had a habit of throwing it open.

Behind the open door, under the angled ceiling, was a short wardrobe and a small desk. Opposite the desk was a door which Joseph correctly guessed was the bathroom. He walked up and peeked inside: a small toilet, a sink and mirror, and a shower. His room turned a hard right, making an L-shape, and there was a bed lined up against the wall.

Standing at the foot of the bed, he could touch the wall above the little desk behind him and almost reach inside the bathroom and touch the toilet. *Small, but good. Perfect, actually. Not too flashy, nothing over the top. Just like me. This will do nicely.*

The ceiling was angled from the exterior wall which had a small window in it. *I didn't think I'd have a view. Shouldn't my room be in the middle of the building?*

Pulling the curtains aside, he realized he was right. His view overlooked a dusty courtyard surrounded by the walls of the hotel. In the center was a small decrepit fountain.

Joseph opened the small wardrobe by the door, happy to find at least one hanger in there. He took off his coat, the leather jacket his father had given him on his eighteenth birthday—the finest piece of clothing he owned—and hung it up. It was tighter around the arms these days, and he couldn't zip it up over his gut anymore, but he still wore it with pride.

Joseph stepped into the remarkably clean bathroom to wash his face. He stood in front of the sink, face dripping with water, only to find there wasn't any soap. Not even one of those small bars wrapped in plastic with the cardboard around it. Glancing into the shower, he hoped to find one there, but it was just as empty. Nor were there any paper towels. He wiped his face as well as he could with his hands, and then rubbed his hands on the back of his pants.

He was startled when he looked up and saw the mirror was fogged over as if he'd just had a scalding hot shower with the door closed. He drew his hand across the glass, but the mirror remained a foggy, milky white. He could barely see the outline of his own reflection when moving back and forth.

*What the hell is going on here . . . ?*

A heavy hand knocked on the door. Joseph—hoping his luggage finally made its way up—rammed his shoulder into the door in his hurry to get out of the bathroom.

"Ow, motherfucker!" he yelled. The knocking carried on. "Yes, yes!"

He swung the door open, smashing it into the angled ceiling, realizing too late that he did what so many others before him had done, only to find the hallway was empty. Leaning out, quickly looking left and right, he thought maybe he heard giggling.

"Hello?"

No answers came from either side of the hallway. *Probably just some kids pulling pranks.*

Joseph closed the door, skipping over the thought of why there would be kids living in an old, run-down hotel.

Sitting on his bed, he grabbed a small piece of paper out of his back pocket. A small photograph, old and worn, with himself on the left, standing next to a beautiful younger woman. Her hair was short and golden, her little nose upturned, her smile just as bright as his. He dragged his fingers across the photo as he gazed into the background. They were standing in front of the Louvre in Paris. It was so long ago, he wasn't sure which year it would have been anymore.

*This is it, you know.* A tear started forming in his eye. *I'll see you soon.*

"Well fuck, I'm going to need my luggage," he said to himself, setting the photograph on the small nightstand. "No point in waiting for them to bring it to me."

Joseph tried the button for the elevator. It lit up, but there wasn't any other reaction. Sensing the déjà vu in how he'd been standing downstairs ringing the bell, he looked over his shoulder in fear that Bryan, the creepy receptionist, would appear behind him.

*If he ever does that again, I'll punch him straight in the mouth.*

Joseph flexed his knuckles. He hadn't been in a fight for more than thirty years probably, but Bryan didn't look like much. If it came down to fists, Joseph would be able to—

*What the hell am I doing?* Joseph shook the thought out of his head. *Planning to fight a guy I've barely met. And for what? He's just—*

"It's not coming."

As prepared as he was, Joseph jolted when someone appeared from the stairs. It was the old man from the fifth floor.

"Didn't mean to scare you, newcomer, I didn't, no." His voice rattled when he spoke, as if the words were getting away from him.

"That's all right, sorry," Joseph said. "Are you sure it doesn't work? I swear I heard it earlier."

"Didn't Bryan tell you downstairs? It doesn't work. Anyway, the stairs are good for you, they are." The old man walked past Joseph and headed down the hallway to the rooms.

*Pretty sure this isn't your floor, old man.*

"Sorry, I didn't catch your name?" Joseph called after him, but the old man didn't reply even though they were barely five strides away from each other. The man continued on without a word.

*Fine, pretend you didn't hear me.* Joseph wasn't one to socialize much anyway, he was just trying to be polite.

THE JOG DOWNSTAIRS was much easier than going up had been. In reverse, the stairwell got bigger as he wound his way down.

Joseph shivered. *You'd think it would be warmer higher up, but my room was freezing. They must only be heating the common areas.*

He walked up to the reception desk and found himself having to ring the bell for service. Again, shuffling could be heard in the backroom by someone who clearly didn't want to help him. He rang the bell again and again, hoping—no, wanting—the person to come out.

*Let's see who can play this game the longest, huh?*

"All right, all right, calm down there, cowboy," a voice said from behind him.

Joseph wasn't startled this time, but he was surprised it wasn't Bryan's slick voice. Instead the tone was the soft and melodious, rolling over him like a warm wind. The bearer of the voice came walking around him, going behind the desk, her lips and eyes smiling at him.

"What can I do for you?" she asked, leaning her elbows on the counter.

Joseph found himself out of words. Her aura was bright against the dreary backdrop of the worn-out hotel. She looked back at him as if she knew him and had longed to see him for years.

"I'm . . . I'm in 704. I was waiting for my luggage."

"Ah, yes. Mr. Podwall. Your luggage has already been brought up." She smiled so hard Joseph would have thought her face hurt yet it looked like it didn't wear on her for a second.

"Are you certain? It wasn't there a moment ago."

"Yes, I'm sure. Must have walked around each other. It happens a lot here."

"But the elevator doesn't work. How could they have gone past me? Is there a set of service stairs?"

"No, I'm sorry, like Bryan told you earlier, the elevator is out of service. Those are the only stairs."

*Yet another person who's overheard my conversation with Bryan.*

"I'm sorry you had to trek down here for nothing, Mr. Podwall. Can I interest you in a drink? On the house, of course."

If Joseph had ever been something, it was a drinker. He'd tried his hand at golf, soccer, the violin for a brief period when he was fourteen, but of all the things he'd ever tried to pick up as a hobby, drinking was the only one that stuck with him. If it wasn't for the other obvious reason, his drinking might have been what finally cracked his marriage.

He took after his father, who had turned him onto whiskey at seventeen. Joseph didn't like it at first, but his father hadn't given up. Every man with a respectable business and a sense of self had to have a good collection of whiskey. It built character. "Never trust a man who turns down a smoke or puts ice in his Scotch," his father had said.

After a while, the habit had stuck with Joseph. He didn't drink himself into a stupor every day, it was just that there was always an occasion. Another glass to fill, and another reason to toast.

"Sure, that sounds great, Miss . . ."

"Alyssa. If you'd like to follow me to the bar, Joe." She left the reception desk, pointing to the lounge across the lobby.

Joseph was so mesmerized by her walk, he let it slide that she'd said 'Joe.' She was beautiful, sure, but not in a flashy kind of way. Joseph wasn't sure he would have turned after her in the street, but here, in the middle of something so old, so run down, there was something about her. Something about the way she moved, the way she talked.

The lounge was dimly lit with mostly brown, wooden décor. Small square tables were dotted about, and a massive bar lined the far wall. The room was absent of other patrons.

"What do you like, Joe?"

"A whiskey would be great. And it's Joseph, please."

"I'm sorry, Joseph." She underlined her apology with a tilt of her head. "But whiskey is so boring. Let me make you a cocktail."

"Sure." He took a seat in the middle of the bar.

"How come you don't like Joe, Joseph?" She laughed as she picked up a few bottles from underneath the bar and grabbed a shaker.

"Joe was my father. Joe and Joseph. He came from a working-class family and built quite a respectable business for himself. Moved up in life, so to speak. He always hated that people still called him Joe. It reminded him of . . . it reminded him of when he was young.

"I'm sorry to hear that," she said lightly, grabbing some ice, lime juice, and a bottle Joseph didn't recognize. She poured generously from the bottle into the shaker. It looked like she was making drinks for three.

*A final drink for the final road. I should have thought of it myself. It's almost poetic.*

"What do you do then, since you're above having a working man's name?" Alyssa winked at him as she continued preparing the cocktail, but he still felt the sting.

"That's not what I meant, but fair point. I'm a travel writer. I just feel like Joseph is more befitting of an adult. And I don't like it when people feel like they've the right to call me something else, to nickname me against my will and shorten my name."

"Makes sense," she said and grabbed a tall glass from a shelf behind her. "They used to call me 'Al' when I was younger, until my teenage years."

Alyssa emptied the shaker into the tall glass, garnishing it with a lemon wedge and a small umbrella.

"Al doesn't sound so good once a girl reaches a certain age." She smiled in the corner of her mouth. "I became Alyssa after that."

Joseph's cheeks reddened as he looked down into the grain of the wooden bar.

Alyssa laughed. "Here you go, Joseph."

He lifted it to his lips and took a careful sip. "What is it?"

"No idea," Alyssa blurted. "Is it good?"

*The best thing I'll drink for the rest of my life.*

"Yeah, not too shabby," he said, swallowing the sickly-sweet drink.

"I'm glad." She leaned on the bar, elbows pointing outward, chin in her hands. "So, what brings a travel writer to The Gate? Writing an article on the oldest, most charming hotel ever?"

Joseph looked around, up and down the bar, and back through the small lobby behind them. "I'm not sure charming would be my first thought, but no. I'm not writing about the hotel. Is it really called The Gate? Where does it say that?"

"Yeah, it is. Didn't you see? There's a great big sign on the wall outside. I can't imagine how you could have missed it."

"Weird. I didn't notice."

Alyssa raised an eyebrow at him. "So, if you're not here to write about the hotel, why are you here?"

"I needed a place to stay as I pass through," he lied. "The Plaza was full, The Grandiose was full. I wasn't too hopeful about finding a place, but when I mentioned The Gate, the driver knew what I meant right away."

*This place is as good as any when I think about it. Better probably.*

"Frank," she pointed out. "He always brings us stragglers who don't have anywhere else to go." A flash of nervousness grazed her face. "No offense."

"None taken," Joseph answered and took another sip of his mystery drink. It wasn't awful, but it wasn't good. "Like I said, I needed a place to—"

"So you're not here for work?"

"Not really, no. Might add a line or two about my stay here though. I'm working for *All Round* at the moment. You know, the magazine. They ask me to go places, I write about them. It's a sweet deal most of the time."

She nodded. "I've heard about it. Don't think I've ever read it. Will I see your name in it if I pick up a copy?"

Joseph grinned and took another sip. "Not in every issue, but in a few, yeah."

He looked up in the mirror behind Alyssa and saw a man walk through the reception area. It wasn't Bryan, that much was clear. Maybe it was the mystery man who hid in the back office.

"I'll make sure to get a copy," she said with a smile. "Maybe if I change your mind, I'll see *my* name in it. You could tell the world about your fantastic stay here."

Joseph couldn't quite put his finger on the look she was giving him. It looked like she was admiring him, maybe even flirting, but then he realized she was eyeing his drink and probably waiting for him to finish. His glass was halfway full, and he decided to down the rest.

"Thanks for the drink. Are you sure I don't owe you anything?"

She shook her head.

"All right, I'll head up and see if my luggage is there then."

Alyssa nodded as Joseph rose from his seat, which left him wondering why she'd gone quiet.

Walking past the reception, he looked and couldn't see Bryan anywhere. But from the back office, he heard a low voice, "Yes, if you could come as soon as you're available. No, we don't know, but several guests have said the same thing. Yes, please."

Joseph couldn't help eavesdropping, the writer inside him eager to understand what the conversation was about.

It wasn't Bryan's voice though, so it must have been the same person who'd been hiding back there all day—a man, older by the gruffness of his voice. The sound of a telephone receiver being put down followed, and Joseph could hear him shuffling around.

Joseph wanted desperately to ring the bell, to force the man to come out and talk to him—to see who the mystery person was—but with his hand hovering over the small silver dome, he decided against it. *Why bother?*

On his way up to his room, Joseph noticed again how out of shape he was, but to his surprise, he didn't feel any of the alcohol. It had tasted of whiskey, hadn't it? Quite much so, and it looked to be a strong drink judging by how much Alyssa had poured from that strange bottle. It had burned his tongue, yet he didn't feel a thing. Not in his head, not in his muscles. He wasn't even swaying the slightest bit. Joseph was the first to admit he could handle his drink, but it had been a while since he'd gone drinking.

*I would have thought a cocktail in the morning would make more of a mark.*

It took him much longer to get to the top floor this time: the stairs went on and on, spiraling upward forever. When he finally arrived on his floor, out of breath and hunched over, he heard the elevator start up again. It whirred and cranked, the heavy sound of old machinery.

*The needle says it's stuck on the first floor, but I can swear it's moving.*

"Liars," he mumbled to himself, closing the door to the stairwell and heading down the hall to his room. It was right there this time—down the hall, a few turns and bends, then up those two steps he remembered.

*Can't be more than forty, fifty steps from the stairwell—what the hell is going on?* He turned to look left and right down the hall. *This place is driving me mad.*

He locked himself inside his room. His key still worked perfectly, almost too well considering the state of the rest of the hotel. And there it was.

His suitcase.

After looking back at the closed door to his room, Joseph eyed the suitcase suspiciously, as if it would reveal some sort of magic to him. *How the hell did you get past me, huh?*

Grabbing the suitcase off the floor, he sat down by the small desk under the angled ceiling and switched on the lamp. The bulb was either damaged or old. It lit up the small space, never mind the rest of the room.

Joseph hadn't brought much, a few shirts, another pair of

pants, and some underwear. His notepad, a few pens, and a small tape recorder for his travel writing were stored away in the compartment in the lid of the case along with his toothbrush, razor, and a bunch of razor blades.

*Finally.*

Taking a blade out carefully, he held it between his index finger and thumb. It glinted in the light of the small lamp.

*Here we are again. Another city, another room. Another escape.*

Unbuttoning his shirt around his left wrist, he rolled it up, just above the elbow. The underside of his arm was riddled with white marks, old cuts mostly, but some new.

His portfolio of scars.

His shaking hand stilled as he held the blade above the wrist. It was cold between his fingers. Taking a deep breath, he moved the blade farther up the arm and cut across the soft skin. First came the pain, that stinging burn he was so accustomed to. Then came the blood, bubbling forth.

Then came the release, a flood of relief as he exhaled.

*No.*

He didn't have it in him to do more than that.

*Not yet.*

Clenching his hand around the cut, hard, he went to grab some toilet paper. With the paper wrapped around his arm, he went over to the nightstand and picked up the photograph again—the one of him and his daughter in Paris.

It still hurt when he looked at Mel, but the cut lessened the pain and grief that threatened to drown him. The few people who had seen the picture often thought it was of him and his wife when they were younger. But no, this wasn't a picture of his ex-wife Susan. She was still very much alive.

Tears didn't roll anymore when he looked at the photograph. It was more anger, some hate.

*I'm so stupid.*

The blood had made its way through the thin, coarse paper toward the German watch at the end of his arm. Another of his father's heirlooms.

He never liked cutting himself. In fact, he didn't even like the pain. It was always his plan that the first cut was going to be the last. Then the next, and then the one after that. But he always stopped short.

Every hotel he stayed in was an attempt to end his miserable life. Instead, he wrote a little story, earned a little money, and moved on to the next. It only left him with more scars, but at least they numbed the pain, if only for a while.

A hard knock on the door, like earlier. Joseph was quick to go and fling it open, another hard bash in the ceiling by the corner of the wooden door. Looking down the hallway, he saw a shadow disappear around the corner. Curious about what might be going on, he decided to chase it.

He rounded a bend in the hallway just in time to see a child lock themselves into the room. A child.

*Fucking kids, I knew it.*

He hammered on the door as soon as he stopped outside it. "Hey!" Another quick succession of hammering with the heel of his hand. "What's the fucking point?"

It wasn't until the third round of knocking that he saw the room number: 708. The room he saw someone lock themselves in earlier.

"Stop hammering on my door, will you?"

Joseph heard crying behind the large green door and figured he had scared them enough. Hopefully they had gotten the message, so he walked back down the hall.

Reentering his room, he was met with the familiar glint of the razor blade. *Did I really leave that on the floor?*

He stared at it for a moment before picking it up. He couldn't remember where else he would have put it. The idea of cutting himself again crossed his mind. It seemed so easy to do when he already had the blade in his hand.

*It could be over. Right here, right now.*

He dragged a finger over the flimsy bandage on his arm. The pain was more than enough already, and he wasn't going to get any braver just yet.

Under the fluorescent light of the bathroom, he carefully removed the thin, sticky toilet paper from around his arm. The bleeding had stopped, the cut already dark red with coagulation. It was thinner than most of his other scars, just a quick little dash. The thickest one was on his forearm, the one and only time he had come close to killing himself. He grazed it with two fingers.

*You were supposed to be my last.*

After their daughter Mel died, he and Susan had never been the same. If she was home and he wasn't drinking, they were shouting. And if they weren't fighting, Joseph was either drinking or making notches in his arm. Susan would be out half the night, probably finding comfort in the company of other men. She never said exactly what it was she was doing, and Joseph was too numb to care.

One morning he had woken in the tub, cold as hell, his skin a pale blue. The cut had stopped bleeding, but he could tell by the bloodstained porcelain and his drenched and crusty clothes that it was serious. It was a wonder he was still alive.

He didn't get braver after that. Not that he didn't want to try again, he always thought about it. One day he would end it all. All those other scars were just practice.

*I've been a coward so far, but The Gate will be the place.*

Looking up at the foggy, milky mirror and over to the shower, he wondered if he should sit down in the tub and get it over with. One gash along—instead of across—both forearms, and he'd be unconscious before he had time to regret it. Or he could go for the inner thigh. Would probably hurt more with the amount of sagging flesh he had there.

*I would have to cut deep, but it would be quicker. Two short minutes and I'd be done with this madness, this disgusting existence, drinking myself uglier and older in a different hotel room every week.*

He flung the razor blade down in the sink. *I'm still a coward. I keep choosing temporary relief over permanent release.*

Joseph stared at the faint outline of himself in the mirror and took a second to wonder what could have caused the glass to become shrouded like it was. That's when he noticed, on the tiles at the top right of the mirror, a fleck of blood. More than a fleck. A spattering.

*Did I do that?*

Brushing his finger over the blood, he concluded no, it couldn't have come from his arm. It was old, dry, and brown. *How have I not noticed it before?* It was quite noticeable, there were—Joseph counted with his index finger—at least seven clearly visible drops.

*Weird.*

As Joseph stepped out from the bathroom, his thoughts were interrupted by a sharp cracking under his heel. Lifting his foot, he saw a small piece of metal and was suddenly glad he hadn't gotten so far as to remove his shoes yet. He bent down to see what he'd stepped on.

Bits of paperclips. Bent yellow metal broken into several pieces. A trail of them lay at the foot of the bed—dozens of small metal sticks.

*Where the hell did these come from?*

He got up and looked around the rest of the tiny room. *Is anything else out of place?*

Joseph jumped as another sound came from the door—not knocking this time, but a rustling of his door handle and a jingling of keys. Before he could settle himself and ask who was there, an old lady swung open the door.

"Excuse me?" Joseph asked, but the woman—a maid, pulling a small, wheeled bucket with a mop in behind her— didn't answer. Humming low to herself, she wheeled her kit straight into the bathroom and promptly began mopping the tiled floor.

"Hello?" Joseph asked again, but the woman either didn't hear him or didn't care to respond. He stared at her for a moment, dumbstruck by the whole situation. She didn't seem to acknowledge him at all.

"Hello? Can you hear me?"

The woman hummed louder, mopping away.

*What the hell . . .*

He turned from the woman, feeling the familiar sting of pain and shame in his arm. He patted the outside of his pockets for his key.

*Guess I could do with one last meal before I go.*

P assing the elevator again on his way down, Joseph noticed it was still whirring. Like it was stuck trying to raise the box from the bottom. *I'll have to remember to double-check if it's still doing that on the ground floor.*

Joseph eyed the elevator suspiciously as he rounded the bottom stair but heard nothing.

"Bryan!" he called out when he saw the pasty-looking kid standing behind the reception. Bryan jumped a little but looked more annoyed than startled.

"Mr. Podwall, I hope you've found the room to your liking. What can I do you for?"

Joseph never understood why people phrased the question that way. *It sounds wrong. Jumbled.*

"Food. What's nearby, and what do you recommend?"

"Our in-house restaurant, of course!" Bryan waved ecstatically across the lobby. "I wouldn't dream of sending you anywhere else, you're just in time for a late lunch. Table for one?"

"Actually, I was hoping to grab some fresh air. Isn't there a nearby diner? Something low-key and—"

"Nonsense," Alyssa's voice said from the bar. "You'll join me for dinner, won't you?" She walked up to the reception and grabbed him by the arm. Joseph flinched and stared down at her hand.

*It looks quite good laced around my arm,* he thought, gritting his teeth as she clenched onto the fresh cut.

"I suppose I could indulge you for a meal," Joseph said in a way he hoped did not sound too flirtatious, considering she was probably young enough to be his daughter. "Where's this restaurant then?"

His arm burned as Alyssa dragged him by it, swirling him around and toward the bar they'd shared a drink in only hours ago. He hoped she wouldn't notice his pained expression.

They stepped into the bar, and Joseph's eyes widened. *What in the world has happened here?*

Joseph could hardly recognize the room. Everything had changed. The low tables which had stood in the dimly lit pub were replaced with long, rectangular tables, each set with white tablecloth and fine silverware. In the middle of the ceiling hung an exquisite chandelier, lighting up the room.

*Whoa.*

"When did this happen?" Joseph asked, pointing up at the ceiling and gesturing out at the completely revamped decor.

"We know how to take care of our guests here at The Gate. Don't let anyone ever tell you otherwise."

*That's not really an answer, but fair enough.*

Alyssa led him to the side of the room, giving him a seat at the end of a long table and taking the one to his right for herself.

Joseph noticed suddenly—as if he'd just woken up—that there were other patrons. The old man who lived somewhere on the upper floors sat by himself. A young blonde woman and a child, who Joseph figured might be the people in 708, shared a table in the corner. And at the far end of the room sat a man in a long trench coat and a hat, opposite a beautiful but stern-looking woman.

Joseph motioned discretely toward the couple so they wouldn't see. "Who are they?"

Alyssa threw her hair over her shoulder as she turned to look at where Joseph pointed, not at all worried that anyone would notice.

"The old man works here. He's our groundskeeper and handyman."

"Really? Maybe tell him to have a look at the elevator?" Joseph smiled slyly, but Alyssa ignored him.

"The young lady and her child have been here for a few weeks. I don't know their story, but the boy's name is Kyle. He's adorable. The two men by the bar are here for business."

Alyssa pointed over her shoulder. Two men, one wide and one thin were drinking coffee, chatted softly to each other, both staring straight ahead into the mirror behind the bar. *How did I not notice them before?*

"And the couple at the end there," she threw a quick glance at the man in the long coat. "Well, the rumors say they're police."

Joseph raised an eyebrow. "And why are they staying here?"

"No one knows." Alyssa shrugged and grabbed two flipped-over glasses and a decanter of water from the middle of the table. "I told Bryan to ask them. He says they didn't say anything, but they're staying here 'until further notice.'" Alyssa's eyes widened and she giggled. "Fascinating, huh?" She poured them both a glass.

"How do you not know what the police are doing in your hotel? What do you mean 'until further notice?'"

"I've heard rumors, but . . . what I mean is they haven't said when they're leaving." She took a sip of water.

*Neither have I.* Joseph looked carefully at Alyssa to see if she would make the same connection. When she didn't, he asked, "What are the rumors then?"

Before Alyssa could answer, Bryan walked over wearing a

large white apron and carrying a silver platter.

*They sure try to make this place look as fancy as possible.*

"Chicken soup," Bryan announced, setting a bowl down in front of each of them.

"Thank you, darling." Alyssa smiled at Bryan. "I think they're investigating," she said before turning back to Joseph.

"What?"

"You know, *investigating*. Figuring stuff out."

"Yeah, I know what investigating is. I mean what would they be investigating?"

"Rumor has it"—she paused, sipping carefully from her spoon—"someone disappeared from upstairs." She smiled at Joseph's cocked eyebrow. "I'm not quite sure who. As I said, rumors, but according to Bryan, a guest went missing."

"You work here. How can you not know if a guest went missing?" Joseph leaned back in his chair, confused.

"I do work here." Alyssa's voice was stern. "But I don't deal with guests personally. Bryan is the only one who knows who comes and goes. Anyway, the guest never checked out, but hasn't been seen for a while. Glenn's been up there to clear out the room. Apparently the police are here to look into it."

"Glenn?" Joseph asked.

"The old-timer." Alyssa threw her head to where he was sitting alone at his table eating his meal. "The groundskeeper."

"No offense, but how can he clear out a room?" Joseph sipped his soup. It gave off an odd aftertaste, but he ate it, nonetheless. It was too late to go looking for anything else. "He looks like he's a thousand years old."

"Age is just a number, Joseph. You should know that, how old are you to be sitting here with me?"

Joseph flushed, sitting straight in his seat. "You were the one who invited me. I don't see why that has—"

She placed a hand on his, laughing. "It's a joke, Joseph! I

have no idea how old Glenn is, but I get your point. Yet he's the one we have. And me and Bryan. And a few others. Anyway, I've heard someone say the person drowned."

"In his room? What did he do, fall asleep in the tub?"

"There aren't any bathtubs," Alyssa answered, and Joseph could tell by the look on her face that she didn't care for his jokes. "And you can drown in any small puddle of water, can't you? Sink, toilet, on your face in the shower. But there's no body."

"What? You said he drowned."

"Yeah, that's the rumor. But the guest is *missing.*"

"Who started the rumor then? Why even speculate how they died if there's no proof, no body? That doesn't make any sense."

"Glenn found all their belongings in the room. Clothing, money, driver's license. It's a real brain twister." She winked at him, carrying on with her soup.

*What? Why is she winking at me? The guy probably left, didn't want to be seen, didn't want any hassle*—Joseph recognized something familiar in his line of reasoning, and his gaze fell on the two police officers. *It'll be good to have them around when I 'leave' this place. Never really thought about who would find me, who would have to go looking for me. By breakfast tomorrow morning, one of them might . . .* His thoughts trailed off, and all he heard was the soft clanking of Alyssa's spoon against her bowl.

"It sure is a brain twister," Joseph said when he finally managed to return to the conversation. "Do you know what room they were in?"

"No idea. One of the top floors, I think. Why?"

"You don't seem worried about these rumors. Don't you want to ask Bryan or Glenn about it? Are you not curious to go check it out? Look for clues?"

Alyssa laughed loudly. The men at the bar cast wary

glances over their shoulders at them.

"Listen to you, Mr. Investigator. And what exactly would we look for? The room's empty, it probably looks just like yours or mine."

"Wait, you live here?"

"Of course I do. I work here." She smiled at him again, but it didn't feel sincere this time. More like a mask she was used to putting on.

"I assumed you came in every morning and left in the afternoon," Joseph said quickly, worried his disbelief might be construed as rude.

"Oh, no. There are so many empty rooms, it's easier for us all to live here. We even get to stay for free. No one really leaves. Except for the guests." She laughed again.

"Fair enough," Joseph said in between spoonfuls of soup. The taste was growing on him. "I'll bet the person disappeared from the fifth floor. I saw Glenn leaving there earlier. Let's have a nose around later."

"I'll have to work the bar later, sorry Joseph."

"You're not working the bar now, who cares?"

She leaned back, a frown taking form on her forehead. "Because this is my lunch. Now, if you'll excuse me, I have to go back." She grabbed the napkin from her lap and threw it on the table before standing up to leave.

"Alyssa, please, that's not what I meant. I'm—"

But she was gone before Joseph could find the right way to apologize. *I've spent less than an hour with the woman, and she already has about as much regard for me as my ex-wife.*

Walking over to Bryan at the reception desk on his way out, Joseph saw a pair of boot heels raised on a table in the back office.

"Got to pull all the weight by yourself?" Joseph asked, pointing behind him, but Bryan only seemed confused when he turned to search for what Joseph meant. "Can you put the lunch tab on my room?"

"Certainly, Mr. Podwall. Anything else I can do for you?"

Joseph fiddled with a toothpick he'd taken off the table. "What can you tell me about the person who went missing?"

"I'm sorry, I'm not sure I get your meaning?"

"Alyssa told me someone went missing. I was wondering what you knew about that."

"Sorry to say, the answer is nothing, sir. Haven't heard about no missing person. Can't help you." Bryan stared at Joseph with a blank look.

Joseph decided to let it go. "Fine. Can you send a few bottles of beer up to my room? I'd ask in the bar, but I'm afraid I offended my lunch companion." *I'm going to need some liquid bravery tonight.*

"Of course, Mr. Podwall. Anything else?"

"Yeah, actually. The elevator." Joseph hitched a thumb toward it in the corner. "It doesn't work?"

"No, I'm afraid not. Like I said earlier, it's out of business."

A smirk appeared on Joseph's face. "You're sure about that?"

"Certain. Is there anything else I can do for you?" Bryan sounded sincere, but looked eager to leave his desk for reasons Joseph couldn't guess.

Joseph gave a small frown. "No, thank you."

He turned and headed toward the stairs. While passing the elevator again, he swore he heard the low whirring of mechanical contraptions. *I wonder why he's pretending to not know.*

On his way back up the stairs, Joseph ran into Glenn. *He hadn't left when I did? How the hell does everyone move so fast?*

"Excuse me?" Joseph walked over, and reached out a hand to the old man. "We met earlier but I forgot to introduce myself. I'm Joseph."

The old man looked Joseph's hand up and down before he slowly took it and shook. "Glenn. A pleasure, indeed." His voice was frail and breaking, his handshake cold and limp.

"Alyssa in the bar told me to ask you. You wouldn't happen to have a master key? Mine's not been working properly in my door upstairs, and I'd—"

"All the keys work properly," Glenn grumbled, turning back toward the hallway. "There's no issue with your key, no there isn't."

As Glenn walked away, Joseph was left speechless in admiration of his simple, no-bullshit reply. *He called my bluff. I'll have to find another way to get into the room on the fifth floor.*

Back in his room, Joseph was happy to see his beers were already delivered. *No way that elevator doesn't work, they're keeping it free for their own use.* He shook his head, opening the first bottle by slamming the cap against the top of the desk.

*Let's be honest, this place isn't winning any awards any time soon, one small scratch in a desk isn't going to make a difference.*

He stared at the small gash he had made in the wooden desk. His gaze moved to his arm. This was how weekends went for Joseph. A cut in the arm to take the pain away from his heart, a beer in his hand to take the pain away from his arm.

He was a surprisingly inconsistent alcoholic, which was probably why he always defended it to his ex-wife.

"One beer a night isn't a problem," he was used to yelling, and he wouldn't be lying. Not all the time, at least. It could be one beer every three days or a bottle of whiskey a night. If he felt like a drink, he'd have it, and Susan could say whatever the fuck she wanted.

He used the first bottle to open the next, and before long, his head was rolling. Holding his bottle out, he gave an invisible cheer.

*Here's to you, Dad, for fucking me up. I like the jacket, and the watch is beautiful, but fuck you, old man. You were a great man, probably, but a horrible father and a shit husband. Thanks for everything.*

He downed the beer in his hand and staggered over to his suitcase and the familiar glint of razor blades.

Joseph woke with a jolt, in a panic, sweat running down his brow. Checking his watch, he saw it was nearly one in the morning. He had slept for about five hours.

*Did someone knock on the door?*

The bottles on the floor explained why he had fallen asleep and why his head hurt so much. Then a low knocking sound came from the door to the hallway.

"Who's there?" he asked with a hoarse cough, tumbling out of bed.

"Open the door, will you?"

He did and found Alyssa standing there. She carried a giant flashlight in her hand, and for the first time, Joseph noticed the lack of lamps in the hallway.

"Fifth floor you said?" she asked with glee.

"I . . ." Joseph had to brace himself by the door frame so as to not tumble out into her. "Yeah, I think so, but there's a problem."

"What?"

"If we go down there, how do we know which room it is? We can't go barging into any old room. I presume there are other guests. And also, how do we get the doors open?"

"Don't you worry about that," Alyssa said with a low giggle, holding a key up to his face. It was made of the same chunky metal as the one to Joseph's room, but the edges were different.

"Don't tell me you have a master key?" Joseph asked.

"Yeah. I grabbed it from the reception."

"Still, that only answers half of my questions. What if we accidentally let ourselves into someone else's room?"

"I take care of that too," she said, patting a large book she bore under her arm. "It's the guest ledger. I know where everyone is."

"What if—"

"Will you just come on already? You were the one who wanted to investigate. Have you changed your mind?"

Joseph's mind flashed briefly with the image of his red arm and a razor blade. He had come to this place for a way out, for an ending, not . . . not for whatever else was going on here.

He shook the image away. *Let's figure this out first.*

"No, sorry, I'm coming," he said, picking up his key from the small desk and closing the door on his way out. "But how do we know there isn't a new guest in the room in question? The room the person went missing from, I mean?"

"Because Glenn's cleared it out this week. The only new guest here is you, and you're not on the fifth floor, are you?"

Joseph couldn't argue with that and cocked his head in agreement. They entered the stairwell about to head down the stairs when Joseph stopped her.

"Do you hear that? How come everyone's been telling me the elevator isn't working?"

"Hear what?" Alyssa asked.

"That!" Joseph insisted, pointing to the whirring elevator shaft. The steady thud and grinding of mechanical gears reverberating from behind the closed double doors boomed in his ears. "It's clearly moving."

"Joseph . . . The elevator isn't making a sound. And who would be riding it now, even if it was working?"

"You're telling me you don't hear that noise? It's

deafening!"

"Is this some kind of joke? Are you trying to get out of going down to the fifth floor? Because if you are, feel free to go back to your bed or your beers or whatever . . . I'm going. You can join me if you want to." Alyssa headed down the stairs, not leaving the conversation open for any further discussion. Shuffling after her, Joseph caught up to Alyssa just as she was about to enter the fifth-floor hallway.

"Wait up," he whispered. He followed her through. The door to the stairwell closed, encapsulating them in darkness.

Alyssa shined the flashlight briefly down each hallway, going back and forth every few seconds. Here the hallways didn't bend and turn quite like they did upstairs. They curved gradually in an arch, and he could have sworn the wallpaper was a different color altogether.

"How come this hotel is so weirdly planned out? It's like the architect hadn't heard of straight lines. And why is it different from floor to floor?"

Alyssa aimed the light at his face, probably bemused by his comments—blinding him and forcing him to shield his eyes with the back of his hand.

"What do you mean? Every floor is exactly the same. If we go down this way"—she swung the light to the left—"we'd get to where you have your room on the seventh floor."

"What?" Joseph realized too late that he'd raised his voice and rephrased himself with a whisper.

"No, we don't. My room is on this side." He pointed down the hallway to the right. "I turn a hard right when I enter the hall, not left."

Joseph could tell by the swinging of the light that Alyssa was shaking her head. "See here?" She shined the light at the wall in front of them. At first, Joseph couldn't quite see what she meant. Then he saw the plaque.

"501 — 520," it read at the top, with an arrow pointing left. "521 — 540," were pointed to the right.

"You're in 704, aren't you? Which means you're on the left."

"Give me that!" Joseph pulled the flashlight out of her hand, more violently than he meant to due to his hangover. He pointed the light down both hallways, at the plaque, then down each hallway again. He swiped a hand across his scalp to calm the feeling of wanting to rip out the last few bits of hair he had. "What the fuck is going on . . ." he muttered. *This place makes no sense.*

"You're probably a bit confused," Alyssa said, taking her flashlight back. "Or maybe it's the drinks."

She hunched down to a squat and laid the large leather-bound book over her knees.

"Let's see." She flipped to the end of the book. "There aren't many guests in the hotel these days, and only a handful are on this floor. Rooms 501, 503, 509, and 517 are the only ones we have to avoid, so let's start at—"

"Or, even better," Joseph said, bending down. "Let's just find the person who was in here who never checked out."

She looked up at him with a look of realization. "You're right, that is better." Alyssa flipped through the pages, confusing Joseph for a moment by going too far—it was difficult to see, even with the light they had—before they eventually found the right entry.

"Doru Amani . . ." she read out loud, tracing the text with her finger.

"Yeah, Doru Amani. Sounds European. Is that a man or a woman?"

"Does it matter?" Alyssa giggled. "Whoever they were, they lived in room 532 and never checked out. According to the register, that room is free now, which means that's our guy."

"All right," Joseph said, struggling back to a standing position. "Lead the way to 532."

They shuffled down the hall in the dark. The fifth floor bent the opposite way, had no steps up or down, and the distance between rooms was shorter. None of it reminded Joseph of his floor.

"Here it is," Alyssa announced, shining the light up at the dark green door in front of them. 532 it read in glinting, gold-plated letters.

"Well, what are we waiting for." Joseph held out an inviting hand. "Ladies first."

Alyssa slid the key into the door and turned it. There was a click, just like the one Joseph heard when he unlocked his own door upstairs. But the door didn't budge when Alyssa tried the handle.

"Give it a little push," Joseph suggested.

"I am, it's not giving."

"Here, let me try." Joseph motioned for Alyssa to get out of the way, grabbed the key and the handle, and pushed on the door with his shoulder. It gave in straight away, sending Joseph headfirst into the room. Like in his own room, the corner of the door slammed into the angled ceiling, making the large dent put there by previous guests even bigger, as Joseph landed haphazardly on the dirty red carpet.

"Oh my God!" Alyssa exclaimed. "Are you all right?"

Joseph rolled over groaning and grabbing his forehead. He was in much more pain than he cared to admit to the younger woman and tried to shrug it off. "I'm fine," he coughed. "Thankfully my face took most of the fall."

Alyssa forced back a laugh.

"Here, let me help you up." She offered him a hand, and with one of his own pushing off the floor, Joseph managed to hoist himself to standing.

"Doru Amani. Let's see what happened to you," Joseph whispered.

The room was exactly like Joseph's but reversed. Small desk under the angled ceiling behind the door and next to a wardrobe. Small bathroom and a single bed on the opposing wall. There was even a window in the same place.

Joseph stared at it for a while, trying to wrap his head around where the window would be facing if they were at the other end of the hotel. Having thought about it for a moment, he realized his head hurt too much—either from the fall or the alcohol—to reach an understandable conclusion. Turning on the small desk lamp he wasn't surprised to see it lit the room just as poorly as his own.

The room was immaculate, completely empty of personal items. It didn't look like there had been anyone there, ever. Glenn sure did his job properly, both clearing out whatever Doru might have left there, and cleaning up afterward.

"Find anything?" Joseph asked.

"Not really, but maybe there's something in here?" Alyssa answered from the bathroom.

Joseph stood in the doorway. The small room was cramped enough as it was with one person, and he wasn't going to make it more uncomfortable by trying to slide in next to her.

"What do you think this looks like?" Alyssa pointed up at the corner next to the mirror.

Joseph's jaw dropped at the sight of a spatter of dark smudges.

"I think it looks like it could be blood. And for some reason, the mirror is completely fogged over. It's weird." *What the hell?*

Joseph pushed himself into the small, cramped space, forcing Alyssa to step into the shower against the far wall.

"Joseph, what the fuck?"

"This is exactly like my room!" Joseph said, dragging a hand over the specks of blood. They didn't disappear. He tried rubbing the fog on the mirrored glass. It didn't go away. "I'm telling you, this is just like this in my room, blood and all!"

Alyssa pushed herself off the wall, squeezing in front of Joseph to look at the smudge of blood. "Every room's the same, it's probably something about the mirrors."

"No, the blood was there as well. Just like this."

"It sounds like a coincidence. You shave in front of the mirror, don't you? You probably cut yourself, and—"

"No, I'm saying it was exactly like this!" He gestured at the specks. "Old, dry blood in this exact same pattern. In this exact spot!"

"Joseph, I think you're overreacting."

Joseph rushed out of the bathroom and motioned to Alyssa. "Give me the light."

She handed it to him as she stepped out of the bathroom. He aimed the light at the floor by the foot of the bed. Crouching down, he saw what he was afraid he would find. Small, bent metal clippings, looking like pieces of paperclips.

"I found these as well in my room." Joseph stood back up and shined the light in Alyssa's face. "Are you messing with me?"

Alyssa frowned. "What? No."

"All of this looks exactly like my room. Is this some kind of joke? Did you do this?"

"Joseph, please." She scowled, shielding her eyes from the light. "You were the one who wanted to come here. *You* convinced *me*, remember?" She huffed. "No, I didn't do this. Why would I?"

"Then why does this look exactly like my room?" He was bellowing again. The hairs on his neck stood up, and his spine tingled with icicles. The light swung around as he looked for other clues—like his luggage or his beer bottles—and landed on the nightstand and a square piece of paper. It was lying face down, but Joseph recognized it immediately: the faded backside, the crumpled corners.

*Mel . . . ?*

A gust blew through the room as he reached for the paper —the paper that was the only picture of Mel, his daughter— lifting it toward the open window.

"No!" he screamed, lunging for the photograph, but it was too late. The photo blew out the window and floated on the breeze all the way down to the courtyard seven floors below.

*Seven floors below?*

Leaning halfway out the window, Joseph scanned the outside of the building around him. He could see the rooftops. He realized he was at the top, like he'd been earlier, standing in his own room.

"This is my room!" he screamed, a nauseating confusion rolled in his stomach.

As the last of the air left his lungs, leaving him with a heavy sense of dread, strong hands yanked him in from the window and forced him back onto the bed.

Expecting to look up at Alyssa's delicate face, he was horrified to see that of an old woman—the face of the maid who'd cleaned his room earlier. She stood over him, muttering something in tones he couldn't understand, her voice growing louder, her mouth gaping wider with every note until she was shrieking at the top of her lungs, filling the small room with violent sound.

Joseph screamed, though he couldn't hear his own panicked voice over hers. He crawled to the end of the bed, tipping out of it onto the floor and scrambling out the door.

"Alyssa!" he called as he ran, tears running down his

cheeks. The vibration of the old woman's howling still rang hard in his head.

*Where did she go? What happened to her?*

Joseph's thoughts were interrupted when he collided with the doors to the stairwell. Happy to find the lights were on in the stairwell, he turned to read the plaque on the wall inside the hall.

It read "701 — 720."

"What the fuck, what the fuck! What the hell is going on?"

The loud whirring of the elevator started behind him. Joseph grabbed the sides of his head with both hands and kicked at the call button on the small golden panel.

"Shut up, shut up, shut up!"

There was still no reaction. Nothing happened. The loud machine still cranked and puffed, pulling the elevator up and down—or trying to, at least.

"I have to get out of here!"

Joseph headed toward the stairs at a sprint. He rounded the corner, and as he descended the second half of the stairs he stepped right out into the lobby.

All the lights were on. Everything was quiet.

"Good afternoon, Mr. Podwall." Bryan smiled. "Shall I find you a table for lunch?"

Joseph stared at Bryan, bewildered. His labored breathing was painful in his chest, his heart still racing. Bryan looked at him as if waiting for an answer.

Alyssa came and grabbed Joseph by the arm, saying something about joining her for lunch. Joseph wanted to scream, to shout and refuse, but he couldn't get a single word out, his feet dragging him unwillingly into the lounge.

"Shall we?" she asked as if nothing had happened. Alyssa led him to the same table as earlier and nudged Joseph into his seat.

"What's going on?" he asked

"Excuse me?"

"Don't give me that shit. What the fuck just happened?"

"I don't know, Joseph, what did just happen? And please, don't use such foul language."

Joseph couldn't believe his eyes, or ears for that matter. They had just been together upstairs in the middle of the night, before Alyssa disappeared on him.

"Bryan?" he called over his shoulder, between a series of deep breaths.

"Yes, sir?"

Joseph had expected to see Bryan behind the reception desk, but he appeared standing on his left.

"When did I check in?"

"Not quite sure, sir. Three, four hours ago? Why, did you need something?"

*But . . . I've been here a day already.* Joseph didn't reply. He just shook his head.

She smiled. "I think it's soup on the menu today."

"Yeah, I know," Joseph muttered while looking around, trying to remember if everything was the same as earlier.

"How could you know?" She laughed as Bryan set two bowls down on the table and left them to their meal.

"We already did this once already."

"What do you mean?" She still sounded like she thought he was kidding, her tone light and playful.

"We sat here and had lunch. You told me about the guest who disappeared from the fifth floor. You told me about Glenn"—he pointed to the older man—"and the two guys drinking beer. We were here, earlier!" Joseph slammed his fist on the table. "And the police—"

That's when Joseph noticed everything was exactly the same. The hotel, the restaurant, the meal, the patrons. Except for the man in the trench coat and the woman.

"Hmm," Alyssa mused, not visibly affected by his violent display. "I don't remember telling you any of that. Are you sure it wasn't Bryan?"

Joseph didn't answer. He was staring intensely at the man in the trench coat. He was facing the other way this time, looking straight at Joseph with glassy eyes and a lopsided smile.

"Excuse me," Joseph said to Alyssa before standing up. He strode over to the couple, noticing that the young woman and the child who had been there the other day were gone. Instead, there was a man with a young girl sitting in the opposite corner, next to where Joseph and Alyssa were seated. *Were they there earlier?*

"Hi." Joseph reached out a hand to the man in the trench coat. The man slowly took it and shook. "Joseph Podwall."

"Clyde Watts," the man said in a gruff voice. "What can I do you for?"

*There it is again, that stupid phrasing.*

Joseph took a seat without asking for permission. He reached out his hand toward the woman. She stared at him with hard eyes and never reciprocated.

Joseph frowned, turning back to the man. "You're police?"

"Now who's gone and told you that?"

"Rumors." Joseph shrugged. "People talk around here, not much else to do. You're investigating Doru Amani's disappearance?"

"What's it to you?"

Joseph hesitated for a second, thinking carefully about how to word himself. "Let's just say I snooped around a bit. Does room 532 ring any bells?"

Clyde pursed his lips. "You haven't been in there, have you?"

Joseph sensed the mood shift. "Why?"

"Have you?"

"Maybe?"

"Did you touch anything?"

"Why, what's going on?" Joseph looked from Clyde to the woman, who still wasn't saying anything. She just kept staring at him with inquiring eyes.

"I'd advise you stay away from Mr. Amani's room in the future, okay?"

Joseph wouldn't have been surprised to receive an earful, but instead Clyde hitched a crooked smile.

"I will, if you can tell me what's going on?"

"I can't, but I'll let you know if we need a third man on this, all right? Room 704 was it?"

"Yeah, sure, I'd be happy to help, but . . . wait, how do you know where my room is?"

"We're the police, Mr. Podwall. It's our job to know things. Now please, I think your company is waiting for you."

Joseph turned to Alyssa, who was eating her soup, not paying him any mind. His own plate sat on the table next to her, waiting for him.

"Sure," Joseph muttered, leaving Clyde and his silent partner to it.

Joseph found his eyes drawn to the young father and his daughter. They were seated in the corner at a small round table pushed up against the yellow wallpaper, not on a large rectangular table like the rest of the dinner guests. The girl was drawing with crayons on a few blank pieces of paper while her dad tried to keep her from going over onto the white table-cloth. In between attempts, he'd take a mouthful of soup, trying to feed her as well, charming her with a train choo-chooing or the swooshing of airplanes. She laughed as the spoon dove toward her face, only accepting an estimate of every third offer. She couldn't be more than five, at most, and her father was young as well.

"What did your new friends say?" Alyssa asked, drawing Joseph's attention away from the table next to them.

"I asked them about Doru Amani and room 532. What the hell is going on, Alyssa?"

"How do you know so much about that?" Alyssa asked, smiling, but nervously.

"Because we went there. After lunch we went to the room. You had the master key, and we looked around, but it . . . it was my room, and I lost the picture of Mel." Joseph had to stop for a calming breath. "Then you disappeared. And the screaming, it was so loud, so I ran downstairs, and now we're here again."

"You're scaring me, Joseph." Alyssa's voice trembled. "I don't get what you're doing, and I don't appreciate it."

"Tell me what the fuck happened then. We were up there, the room was mine, then I lost the photograph of . . ."

It suddenly struck Joseph that he hadn't been back to his room since. *Is it really missing then?*

He hadn't seen any of his other possessions in that room, but the photo was there, and it had disappeared.

"The photograph of?" Alyssa asked.

"Mel . . . Melanie. She was my daughter. I always carry a picture of her, and . . . well, now I fear I've lost it. I should go back up and check." Joseph was about to push the chair away from the table, when Alyssa grabbed his hand.

"I think you should eat first. At least do that. It sounds like you've had a nightmare or . . . I don't know, but eat first, okay?"

"Or what?"

"You should eat before it gets cold—"

"Or what, Alyssa? Just say it. Was it a joke?" Joseph realized he'd never checked if it was night when he'd woken up in bed after all the beers. He had just gone by his watch. Someone could have played a joke on him, turned the lights off and—

"Well, I say this simply as a little fun-fact, a little tidbit of local lore, but . . ."

"But what?"

"Some say The Gate is haunted."

Joseph scoffed, drawing back. "There's no such thing as ghosts."

"No, that's not what I mean. Some say the hotel itself is haunted. As in . . . I don't know. Weird things have been known to happen. To the rooms, to the people who stay here."

"Like with Doru?"

"I was referring to you." Alyssa cocked her head, indulging in another spoonful of soup. "Tell me about her."

"Who?" Joseph didn't like that they were changing the subject.

"Your daughter."

"Mel?" His spine tingled, and his jaw clenched. He wanted to continue talking about what had happened, about upstairs. But at the same time, the thought exhausted him.

"She was the best. There aren't enough words to describe her. The kind of little girl who could put a smile on your face, you know?" He gazed at the young girl sitting in the corner of the room and smiled to himself. She wore her hair just like Mel.

"She grew into this beautiful woman, much too early if you ask me. Short, bright hair, and eyes that smiled at everyone."

"She sounds gorgeous."

"She was." His eyes drew away from Alyssa's. "She didn't live past nineteen, unfortunately."

*Why am I telling Alyssa this? She doesn't need to know.* He'd hardly ever told anyone about Mel, and now he'd told a perfect stranger in an old hotel.

"What happened?" Alyssa asked in between spoonfuls of soup.

"She was—" Joseph took a deep breath. "She was killed. Murdered, I suppose. A stabbing. They never caught the guy who did it, and . . . the details are unclear."

Joseph's wrist seared with pain. *I can't keep going on like this,* he thought as his hand grazed over the fresh cut under his shirt.

Her hand was on his again, her face still kind with joy, but not smiling anymore.

"I'm so sorry, Joseph." She looked down at her soup before pushing it away. "You know, I'm done eating, how about you?"

"Yeah, I'm not hungry."

"Let's go see if we can't find that photograph, okay? You

know, you've probably had a panic attack of some sort, I've heard they can be quite fickle."

"I . . ." Joseph didn't know what to think. Which was worse: that it had happened or that it was all in his head? "Don't you have to work or something?" Joseph asked, remembering her reaction earlier—whenever it was—when he'd suggested she leave her post. "Work the bar?"

"No. Not now." She laughed. "I'm not on the clock until much later. Come, let's go."

They walked out as they'd come, arm in arm, Alyssa guiding him through the dining room, toward the lobby and the stairs.

Joseph caught Bryan's gaze as they walked past the reception, all smiles and greasy hair. Bryan nodded courteously at them as they started the stairs, a sly gleam in his eyes. *What is he thinking?*

Passing the fifth floor, Joseph stopped her.

"Just a second, I want to check something." He walked over and opened the door halfway. The lights were on now, brightly lit, and he could see the golden plaque clearly. Rooms one through twenty on the right, the rest on the left.

*Just as I thought.*

"Sorry, never mind," he said, rejoining Alyssa on their walk up the stairs.

He spent the last remaining steps thinking about why Alyssa had offered to come with him. Did she have ulterior motives for being in his room? To look for the photograph, sure, but what if it wasn't there? Or even yet, what if they found it?

He grazed a hand over his arm, sending a flare of pain through him.

"Here we are," Joseph announced, searching for his key in his pockets.

"Looking for this?" Alyssa grinned. At first, Joseph thought it was the master key from earlier, and the words stuck in his throat. If the key was real, then everything Joseph had experienced must have happened.

"You left it on the table, I grabbed it for you."

It was his key—704 clearly stamped into the handle. Joseph grabbed it from her slender hands and unlocked the door. It opened without issue, not like on the fifth floor.

Inside, everything was as he'd left it. His luggage was on the small desk, the opened and empty bottles of beer were next to his case, plus some on the floor.

"Explain the bottles," Joseph said, pointing to the floor. "I ordered these last night. And I drank them all before you came and got me."

He remembered he left his razor blade in the sink earlier —or was it yesterday?—and quickly shuffled in and grabbed it.

*She doesn't need to know about that.*

Hiding it in the palm of his hand, he thrust the blade into his suitcase, stuffing it underneath some clothes while Alyssa was contemplating the bottles.

"Hey, everyone likes a drink now and then," Alyssa said, standing at the bend of the L-shaped room, where Joseph's bed ended.

"Yeah, sure, if that's what you want to call it. But what about the beers? When did I drink all of these if I haven't already been here for a day?"

"Like I said, Joseph, the mind can play tricks on you. Particularly if you had a couple of bottles for breakfast, don't you think?" She smiled and quickly changed the subject. "Your photograph. Where did you lose it?"

Joseph rubbed his eyes, wondering if Alyssa might be right, and he really had been drunk for breakfast. Days could certainly blend together when he was on a bender—maybe the opposite could happen as well.

"Is . . . is there anything on the nightstand? I thought I left it there."

"Nope," Alyssa said, bending down to look underneath it and under the bed. "Sorry," she said from the floor. "I can't see it anywhere."

"Then I think it flew out the window, but really, Alyssa, you don't have to—"

"No, I want to. It's no bother at all. Let's see where we are." She opened the window with a bang, slamming it against the top frame as it unstuck from itself.

Alyssa put her hands on the ledge and leaned out. "I can't see the photograph, but you're facing the middle courtyard. It's not really in use anymore, but I can take you out there. Maybe we'll find your photograph there?"

"That . . ." Joseph hesitated. He wasn't sure if he should drag Alyssa into more unfathomable events. He wanted to talk about last night, to try and understand, but he also really wanted to find the photo of his daughter. He *needed* it if he was going to follow through with his plan.

"That would be great, if you're sure you're up for it."

"Of course, let's go."

Joseph contemplated the razor blades in his suitcase before he left, his arm flaring up with pain as he did.

*I'll come back to this later—to all of it, when I know Mel's photo is safe.*

Walking past the elevator in the stairwell, Joseph stopped briefly on the carpeted floor to listen for any sound coming from the elevator shaft. It was silent now—finally.

"Are you coming?" Alyssa called up at him from around the bend in the stairs.

"Yes, sorry."

By the reception there was a door. Not the one that led to the back office—where Joseph swore he still heard someone moving about—but at the other end, right next to the elevator.

Alyssa fished out a small golden key. It wasn't like the room keys Joseph had seen so far. He presumed all employees carried a set of keys. Alyssa worked in the bar after all, even if she spent most of her time sneaking around with Joseph.

"This leads to the kitchen, the staff rooms, the boiler room downstairs, aaaand . . ." she dragged out the word like she was announcing the winner of a contest.

"The courtyard?" Joseph asked.

"Ding, ding, ding! You're correct!"

She led him down a dark hallway, abnormally wide and high under the ceiling with the same awful décor as the rest of the hotel. There were a few light fixtures on the walls, but none above them. Joseph got an unnerving feeling of being led into a hospital, or an operating room, or . . .

*A morgue.* That's what it reminded him of. The cold, never-ending hallway of a morgue. He'd been in one before, and it had been the worst experience of his life.

"It's through here," Alyssa said as she exited the hallway into a large, domed hall. It looked like a ballroom—a dusty, forgotten ballroom.

"Woah, what's this?" Joseph asked, stopping to take it all

in. A small podium stood at the end of the large room, looking like it could have been a stage for a handful of people. Huge windows let in a lot of light, more than anywhere else in the hotel.

"Just an old room we don't use anymore."

"Why not? Why don't you have dinner in here? This is much nicer than that dreary lounge by the bar. No offense."

"None taken," she said, but her pursed lips betrayed her. "I'm not sure. I think there was a fire, and it's been put out of use. Anyway, come here, we're going this way." Alyssa waved him over to a huge set of wooden double doors.

Oak, Joseph guessed, though he had no real idea other than that they looked like they were made of thick, heavy wood.

Alyssa fished out another keychain, older looking this time, with bigger, chunkier keys. She flipped through the old keys, stopping on the fourth.

"Let's see," she said and slid the key into the massive door. It clanked and turned with a metallic thud. The door creaked open as Alyssa leaning on it with all her weight.

The smell of sharp, cold air hit Joseph's nose. They found themselves in the courtyard Joseph had seen from his room. It was almost circular, even though all the building faces were straight. Two parts of the hotel stood at an angle to the rest. Joseph supposed it was a hexagonal shape, but again, slightly off like everything else.

Shrubbery lined the border of the courtyard, and what Joseph could only imagine used to be a fountain adorned the middle. It had a concrete circular base, but the middle spire where the water would have come up was shattered, and the broken pieces were missing.

Off to the side was a small staircase made of hewn stone, leading up to a small door about six feet off the ground.

Directly opposite the stairs were two doors, mirroring those Joseph and Alyssa had come through.

"This isn't going to take long," Joseph mused. "It looked bigger from up there." He pointed up at where he presumed his room was, realizing he had no idea which side it would be on. In fact, it didn't even look like there were seven floors.

"Let's have a look around then," Alyssa said, following the wall to the left. Joseph went right.

It didn't take him long to find the photograph. It was lying there, in a bush, just as they theorized. The paper was a bit moist, but not so wet that it wouldn't dry up and look like new —or at least like it had before.

Joseph breathed on it and cleaned it off on his shirt. He smiled. Mel smiled back at him from Paris. *How many years ago was it?*

"Alyssa? I found it!" he called out, stepping over shrubbery into the middle of the courtyard, but finding it empty. *She was right here a second ago, wasn't she?*

Stepping up on the concrete ledge of the fountain, he tried to get a better overview of the courtyard. How could she have disappeared? It wasn't as if there were any places to hide.

He walked across the cracked concrete to the opposite staircase and the large bush beside it. Maybe Alyssa was hiding behind it, but as Joseph stepped up, it became obvious she wasn't there. He walked back around the bush and took the seven steps up the stone stairs to a small door. A service entrance, he guessed.

Assuming Alyssa could have gone through there to be funny or play games with him, he tried the door. It didn't budge. It felt loose on its hinges, as if it would open easily. If it wasn't locked.

"Alyssa? Where the hell did you go?" he yelled. No

response. He pulled his coat tighter. It had grown cold in the time he had been out here.

He jogged over to the opposing double doors and tried those as well, only to realize they were also locked.

"Well, I found the photograph! I'm leaving now if you care to join me."

He walked back toward the wooden doors, half-expecting Alyssa to pop out of the fountain. There was probably some hidden mechanism, a crawl space or winding staircase. Jumping out to scare him felt like something Alyssa would do. He grabbed the handle of the door to drag it open, and at the same time, he felt it swing toward him.

"There you are—" he stopped when he realized it wasn't Alyssa behind the door. It was Clyde the police officer and his silent partner.

"We have some questions, Joseph," Clyde said.

Joseph stared, dumbfounded. Their eyes were hard, their faces set with a grim seriousness.

"Come with me," Clyde said, motioning for Joseph to follow them back through the hotel to the dining room. Before he knew it, Joseph was sitting at their table in the lounge.

"Mr. Podwall," Clyde began. A diplomatic tone permeated his voice. "Does the name Alyssa Tiller, mean anything to you?"

"I don't know about Tiller, but if you're talking about the bar-maiden named Alyssa, then yeah. I was just outside with her, why? Has something happened?"

Clyde unfolded a small notepad in his lap and took a pencil from inside his long coat. "You're saying you were outside with Alyssa? When was that?"

"Just now." Joseph gestured with open palms toward where they had walked through the reception. "Literally minutes ago."

"You're certain we're talking about the same person here, Mr. Podwall? Alyssa Tiller."

"I don't know if her last name is Tiller, like I said, but her first name is Alyssa. She works here." Joseph turned to point at the bar in frustration. "You must have seen her dozens of times. Why are you asking?"

"Mr. Podwall, Alyssa has been missing for four days. Now, the gentleman at the bar said you were seen having lunch with her the other day, and—"

"Wait, what? Four days? I was with Alyssa less than half an hour ago! We were out in the courtyard. I haven't even been here for four days for fuck's sake. You saw me with her earlier!"

"Watch your language," the woman next to Clyde said. Her voice was rough and hoarse, and her outburst made a lock of black hair fall over her forehead. She straightened in her seat and carefully pulled the hair back with a delicate finger.

"She talks," Joseph said with raised eyebrows. "Well, excuse me, but someone's got their timeline messed up. I was with Alyssa only minutes ago."

"Where is she then?" Clyde asked.

"She disappeared."

"I'm sorry, Mr. Podwall. You're saying you were with the woman just minutes ago, and now you're saying she disappeared?"

"Yeah, we were out in the courtyard. I bent down to pick up this photograph I'd dropped, and when I looked up, she was gone."

Clyde looked nonchalantly down at his notes, gazing over at his partner with a contemplative look. Her already furrowed brows scrunched closer together.

"That sounds odd, because Bryan in the reception assures us that Ms. Tiller hasn't shown up for work the last four days, and that you, in fact, were the last person to see her when you had lunch." Clyde rummaged through his notes. "Five days ago."

"You must be fucking joking. Did she put you up to this?" Joseph chuckled. "Like I said, I haven't been here for that long, I checked in today or yesterday, and I—"

"You don't remember when you checked in?" Clyde asked with a cocked eyebrow. "Because according to the receptionist, you've been here for a week."

A shiver ran down Joseph's back, his eyes falling out of focus. "That's not . . ."

Sweat dripped down his hairline, picking up speed along with his racing heart. *A week? But I checked in today. Or was it yesterday? What the fuck is happening?*

Joseph sighed, inhaled deeply, and thought for a moment. Everything depended on whether the events of the last night had been real or not. If they were, that would make it tomorrow already, but if they weren't, and he'd gone down for lunch for the first time today, then he'd only been there for hours.

"The beer!"

"Excuse me?" Clyde asked.

"Yesterday I had lunch, brought a few bottles of beer up to my room and fell asleep. I woke up in the middle of the night, and me and Alyssa went out—" Joseph rambled, trying to make it sound coherent, mostly for himself. He wasn't crazy. There had to be an explanation for all this.

"When I ran back downstairs in the middle of the night, it was lunch again. But I saw the bottles up there when I was in the room with Alyssa. Which means that at least that much must have happened!"

Clyde and the woman gaped at him.

Joseph shot up from the table and ran toward the stairs. He thought he heard Clyde and his partner clamber after him. Perhaps the interview wasn't over yet, but he didn't care. Joseph was done.

*Five days is bullshit. I haven't been here that long.* But if the bottles he drank last night were real, then he had at least been here for two days, which in turn meant that someone, somehow, was playing games with him.

*The hotel isn't haunted, that's impossible.*

Alyssa had been downstairs in the courtyard half an hour ago. There was no way she had been missing.

Joseph reached the landing of the seventh floor drenched in sweat.

*Got to count the steps next time, all this cardio has to count for something,* he thought as he gasped for air and made his way to his room. Joseph unlocked the door and almost managed to grab it before it slammed into the ceiling, but he wasn't fast enough. Another dent in the steadily growing wound.

Clyde and his partner arrived just moments after Joseph stepped into the room. His suitcase was there, his bed like it had been since he arrived—slightly ruffled. There was no sign of the beer bottles.

"What the fuck? Someone must have cleaned up in here, I drank six beers last night."

"Doesn't look like you did, Mr. Podwall." Clyde stepped through, doing a round inside the room and checking the trash cans. "Unless you hid the bottles yourself. No one's been in here to tidy up, the bed is still unmade." He peered into the bathroom. "Looks like there's blood in the sink. Care to explain?"

*I put my razor blades away—at least that's real.*

"I cut myself while shaving," Joseph said.

"Now, that would sound plausible if you were clean-shaven. But you're not." Clyde cocked his head. "I'd say it would take me at least three days to grow that amount of stubble."

"Listen, I don't know what happened to Alyssa, and I certainly haven't been here for a week! I came yesterday, I think, but I *know* I saw Alyssa earlier today." Joseph looked up at them both, nostrils flaring. "Hell, you both saw Alyssa today! She was sitting at the table with me during lunch, eating soup. You must have noticed, because you said my company looked lonely or something."

Clyde frowned, a grimace that looked painful to hold for the otherwise calm man. "You must have shared a table with more than one person, because I didn't see Alyssa, did you?" He turned to his female companion who remained as stoic as always.

She shook her head slightly. "No, we only saw the little girl. Your daughter, I presume. The one who was drawing."

"What? That wasn't us, I was there with Alyssa, and I—"

Dark spots burst into Joseph's field of vision like he was staring down the length of a tunnel. His voice broke. his tongue swelled. His arms flailed as he tried to catch himself but the floor came rushing up to meet him. Clyde's strong arms wrapped around his chest.

"There, there," he heard as the world went dark around him.

J oseph came to on his bed. Clyde and the woman hovered over him. The inside of his room—his desk, his things, his door—was a blur as they helped him outside.

He swore the hallway from his room was longer, like it had been the first time he came up to his room. Turning strange ways and bending awkwardly.

Joseph swayed and staggered. He could feel Clyde grab him while the woman unlocked the metal gate to the elevator, drew it aside, and pressed a button on the inside panel. Joseph recognized the whirring and clanking noise, and before he knew it, he was standing in the lobby. His feet were heavy, like they had walked the stairs, but the sound of the elevator still rang in his head. It worked.

Bryan stared at him from behind the reception desk—the unnaturally worried look on his face didn't suit him—as the three entered the bar. The room was different again. No dining tables, no white tablecloths. There were round secluded tables and booths along the walls, the kind you found in old diners.

*How did they put the booths in?*

"This is Marcia," Clyde said, finally introducing his partner now that they were settled at one of the round tables. Joseph stared off into the wallpaper behind them. He might have been interested in her name a few hours ago, but right now breathing was the only thing he could concentrate on. He struggled to draw air. It was all so much. It burned in his wrist.

"Can I . . ." Joseph was barely whispering, his usually steady voice on the brink of tears. "Can I see some identification?"

Both Clyde and Marcia produced their badges willingly. Detectives, both, with the local police. They weren't lying. So why were they saying all the things they were saying?

"Mr. Podwall, where's your daughter?"

Joseph sniffed. "My daughter's dead."

"The girl who was here with you earlier?"

"That's not my daughter. I wasn't here with my daughter. She died years ago. She was nineteen."

"Who was the girl then?"

"I don't know."

"But you had lunch with her." Clyde said, twisting in his seat.

"No. I didn't."

Alyssa's tale of the haunted hotel rang in Joseph's head as he stared at the wall behind Clyde. The red floral pattern looked like it was spinning, moving, almost alive.

"I ate with Alyssa. Then we went upstairs to look for a photograph of my daughter, which I thought I'd lost. We found it in the courtyard earlier. Then Alyssa disappeared."

"When did you lose the photograph?" Clyde asked.

"Last night, on the fifth floor."

"Why were you there last night?"

"Alyssa and I went to Doru Amani's room."

"You locked yourself into someone else's room? In the middle of the night?"

"Yeah, the missing guest's room. I told you guys this earlier. We wanted to investigate the disappearance."

"Of Alyssa?"

"What? No, of Doru Amani."

Clyde opened his mouth, but Marcia cut him off with her

growling voice. "Why did Alyssa help you look for your photograph in *your* room if you lost it on the fifth floor?"

*How do I explain that?*

"Because the room was . . . it was my room. Or so I thought. Anyway, if I hadn't lost it there, then it would still be in my room upstairs, but it wasn't, so we went looking in the courtyard."

"Do you have the picture?" Clyde asked.

With shaking hands, Joseph produced the photo from his shirt pocket and pushed it across the table for Clyde to see. He was on autopilot, just doing as he was asked. Tears began rolling, leaving salty streaks down his cheeks.

"Mr. Podwall . . ." Clyde sounded hesitant as he turned the picture around toward him. "You're saying this is a picture of your daughter, yet at the same time, you're saying it's not the little girl you had lunch with yesterday?"

Joseph took a second to fully understand the sentence he'd just heard and looked slowly down at the photograph. He jerked back violently, almost tipping off his seat. It wasn't the picture of his teenage daughter and younger self, but a picture of the couple he'd seen in the lounge—the man in his twenties with the young girl. The child with the crayons. Joseph grabbed his head with both hands, staring at the picture, his eyes tearing up again.

"That's . . . I . . ."

"Mr. Podwall, this is you, isn't it?" Clyde pointed to the man, and it wasn't before now that Joseph recognized his younger self in the picture.

"I—yes, that's me."

"And is this your young daughter, who we saw you with here yesterday?" Clyde's finger shifted toward the little girl. Blonde locks of hair in her eyes, her face more smile than anything. It took Joseph longer than with himself, but yes, it was a young Mel he was looking at. Young, sweet Mel.

"Yes," he whispered. "Yes, that's her. But I met you here today, not yesterday, and I—"

"Where's your daughter now? She wasn't in your room." Clyde's eyes appeared understanding, even though his words were harsh.

Marcia's eyes were still, like the rest of her, only revealing a hint of contempt.

"Like I said, she's not here."

"Because she's dead?" Clyde asked with disbelief.

"I . . . yes."

"Mr. Podwall, we saw your daughter here yesterday. Are you saying she died after that?"

"No, she . . ." Joseph couldn't find the words. He wasn't sure it mattered if he did. *Have I lost my mind? Maybe Alyssa was right; maybe this place is haunted.*

Looking at the picture now, he recognized Mel. Of course, it was Mel. But had it been Mel sitting there earlier? Drawing with crayons?

"What's the purpose of your stay?" Marcia asked with careful enunciation.

"Traveling through," Joseph muttered. The cut on his wrist seared as he lied. "I'm a travel writer. I write for magazines about the places I go." He wasn't about to tell them he came here to kill himself, only to end up with a cut on the arm and a heavier conscience.

"Traveling where?" Clyde asked.

"Like I said, *through.*"

Clyde turned to Marcia, trying to whisper but Joseph overheard him telling her to go up to Joseph's room and look for any sign that a girl had been staying there.

"No, you can't search my room!" Joseph resisted, thinking

about the bloody razor blade they would find in his suitcase. "I won't allow it. I won't give you my key."

"We already have your key, Joseph," Clyde explained, and Marcia held it over her head as she walked away.

"No, but you—" Joseph lurched after Marcia, but Clyde grabbed him by the arm.

"Sit back down." His voice changed to a determined strictness as opposed to the nonchalant carelessness from earlier. "We're going to talk for a little while longer." He turned and gestured to Bryan at the reception. "I'm not asking."

"Sure," Joseph said, staring into the tabletop.

Bryan came over, and Clyde asked for two cups of coffee. He asked if Joseph would like anything in his, but Joseph didn't reply. Clyde asked for cream and sugar.

"So, Joe. You don't seem to know where either your daughter or Alyssa is."

*Don't call me Joe.*

"No, I don't. My daughter isn't here. She died nearly twenty years ago."

"She was alive yesterday, Joe. That doesn't make any sense."

"I know it doesn't, but that's the way it is. A lot of things don't make any sense in this place, haven't you noticed? I saw her body at the morgue, we had a service, and we put her to rest in a beautiful little secluded graveyard near where her grandparents live."

"Pardon me if I have a hard time believing that."

"Well, it's true. My daughter's not—"

"Who was the little girl you were with then? And where's Alyssa?"

Joseph sprang from his chair, leaping backward before Clyde had time to react. "I'm telling you I wasn't here with a little girl! There was this young man, and I was sitting there."

Joseph pointed behind him to where he and Alyssa had shared their lunch. "And I'm probably more than twice his age, and—"

"You can't be more than twenty-five."

That took the words out of Joseph's mouth. Joseph slowly turned toward the bar. He peered through the shelves, past the bottles lined side-by-side, to stare into eyes in the mirror.

They weren't his. He took a step closer, studying the face slowly revealing itself above the half-empty bottles. It wasn't that of an aging, balding, fat man. He was young again, young with tan skin and thick hair. It felt like an illusion at first, as if someone else was looking back at him through a window, not a mirror. Until he looked down at his hands. His stomach became a dark, bottomless pit, and his body flushed with cold sweat from the back of his head down to his ankles. He toppled backward, falling over the table where Clyde still was sitting.

"Jesus Christ!" Clyde yelled, scurrying over to catch him, but Joseph crashed over the table and landed hard on the floor.

"Stay away from me!" he screamed at Clyde, crawling back to his feet, running toward the lobby and the stairs.

"What's going on?" Bryan shouted as Joseph ran past him, Clyde in tow, up the stairs.

Joseph couldn't fathom whose body he was in, but it both looked and felt younger as he traversed the steps two at a time. Third floor, fourth floor, it was going so quickly, like he was running downhill. Clyde was already far behind him, but Joseph knew the victory would be short-lived if he ran straight into Marcia's arms upstairs in his room.

*Fifth floor, maybe room 532 is still open? I certainly didn't lock it up.*

He bolted through the door separating the hallway from the stairwell and hunkered down behind it. Planting both palms on the bottom of the polished wood stopped it from swinging back and forth. Seconds later, he heard Clyde come lumbering up the stairs, turn around on the landing and carry on upstairs.

After a few breaths, his body felt reinvigorated enough to carry on, but he made sure to take his time, double-checking which way he had to go. Joseph couldn't quite remember—or believe—the events of the previous night, but he knew he and Alyssa had gone left, against his own rational thought. Looking up at the golden plaque, it seemed such was the case this time as well. "521 — 540" was right again, not left.

"Right it is then. Damn haunted hotel bullshit," he muttered.

Grabbing the door handle to 532, Joseph's stomach sank. It wasn't open. Of course, someone would have locked the door since he'd been there last.

Joseph was about to turn and leave when he remembered how sticky the door had been the previous night. It had taken the force of his whole body to open it. Grabbing the handle tighter, he gave it another push, smashing the corner of the door against the ceiling.

"There you are. What took you so long?"

Alyssa was sitting there, bathed in the light of the small desk lamp in the tiny little room identical to Joseph's own upstairs. She looked up from a stack of papers in her hands. A piece of cloth lay on the desk next to her.

"Alyssa?" Joseph uttered after a moment's pause, walking inside the small room, swinging the door shut. "You're here?" He was dumbstruck. She looked like nothing had happened.

"Of course I am. Where else would I be?"

"You disappeared in the courtyard, when we were looking for my photograph!"

"What?" She smiled, putting an elbow on top of the chair's

backrest and turning halfway toward him. "When were we in the courtyard?"

"I . . . In the . . ." Joseph stumbled for words. "Don't you remember? After lunch earlier, we went to look for my photograph. First in my room, then in the courtyard?"

"No, we didn't, silly. After lunch I went back to work." She crossed her arms and gave a frown that looked half-playful. "I distinctly remember, because you offended me. Bryan came and picked up a case of beer for you, which they sent to your room, and then I came and picked you up in the middle of the night." She shook her head, checking her watch. "That was twenty minutes ago."

"What?" Joseph braced himself against the door to the bathroom, pinching his eyes hard. *What is going on?*

"I . . ." Joseph needed to understand, but his brain couldn't wrap itself around where to begin. "Whose room is this?"

"This is Doru Amani's room, the guest who disappeared." Alyssa went back to studying her papers. A smile caressed the corner of her mouth. "You sure you're all right? You were the one who said we should go up here after all."

"Yeah, I'm fine, I'm—I think so."

He went into the bathroom, closing the door. It suddenly dawned on him that Alyssa hadn't mentioned his appearance or been freaked out that he looked different, so he went to look at himself in the mirror.

But he couldn't, because the mirror was still fogged over. He had to take Alyssa's reaction as evidence that he looked like his same old self, and judging by his worn and wrinkled hands that seemed to be true.

Joseph splashed his face with water before going to sit on the bed. He tried to wrap his head around what had happened when.

"So we never went to the courtyard?" He stood up to look

out the window. The courtyard was right there, encircled by the wall of the hotel and the broken fountain in the middle. To Joseph's relief, when he looked across the courtyard to the other side of the hotel, he counted seven floors in total.

"Nope, not me. Maybe another of your nighttime companions joined you?" She chuckled, and Joseph couldn't quite understand if the joke was about herself or him.

"You picked me up from my room just now? 704?"

"Yup."

"Had I been drinking? Were there beer bottles on the floor?"

"Yeah, I think so. I assumed that's why you stepped out to get some air?"

*Am I just too drunk? Did I pound six bottles before we went down here and imagine everything about the photograph and the courtyard?*

"When you said, 'earlier'"—Joseph wanted to ask her about what she'd said about the hotel being haunted, but she'd said that after the second lunch, not the first, so for her it might not have happened. "Has there been weird things happening at this hotel before?"

"What do you mean?" Her eyes didn't leave the papers.

"Weird things. Unexplainable things, like . . . ghosts?"

"You're into that kind of thing, aren't you?" She shrugged. "Many people have claimed the hotel is haunted. Every old building is, isn't it?"

"So, things have happened here? With other guests?"

"Not to my knowledge, no. Why are you suddenly so interested in this? Is The Gate getting to you, Joseph?" She let out an amused laugh.

The conversation didn't jog her memory, so Joseph moved on. "What are you reading, by the way? Did you find something Doru left behind?"

"Yeah, these are some notes from his time here." She held a few of the pages she'd already read above her head for him to grab. "They detail his stay. He's counting days until . . . until he gets to leave, it seems. It's all a bit floating and abstract. He mentions talking to me at my bar, sharing what he describes as *deep personal thoughts*. But I can hardly remember the guy's name, or that he sat at my bar."

Joseph scanned the pages he was given and the ones she was currently reading. Alyssa was right. Most of it was keeping track of days, how long since he'd arrived, and how his living there was a *meaningless, worthless experience*, and *a waste of a perfectly good life*.

"Looks like our mystery guest was overwhelmed in here," Joseph said. *I can certainly understand why.* "Also sounds like he didn't want to leave."

"Maybe he couldn't?" Alyssa proposed.

"Why not?" Joseph laughed, his voice sounding uncontrollably nervous. He slumped down on the bed again, his head suddenly throbbing. "What would stop him?"

Alyssa faced him in her chair. "Wouldn't necessarily be something that kept him from leaving, but what if something kept him from returning home? Or from going where he needed to go?"

Joseph shrugged. "I suppose, but there must be better places than here to come to?"

"You couldn't find any, could you?" She laughed and stood up.

*Yeah, but this was only supposed to be a layover for me.*

"Come. I found something else, now that I think of it."

She walked into the bathroom, and Joseph joined her. They had to stand intimately close to be able to fit inside the tiny room. Alyssa went all the way into the shower, pulling the curtain away.

She pointed a finger at a few of the tiles. "Look here."

It was difficult to see, even with the fluorescent lights coming from the bathroom ceiling.

"Didn't you have a flashlight with you?" Joseph asked.

"What? No, why'd you think that?"

"Never mind," Joseph said. *Another figment of my imagination.* "What am I looking at?"

"These red marks. Tally marks. Four in a line, one across. Over and over again, almost nine times."

"He was counting something?"

"Looks like it," Alyssa said, carefully dragging her fingers over the marks. "I'm guessing days. If I'm correct in thinking it's how long he stayed here, he's been here for forty-three days."

"Is that important?" Joseph asked.

"Important is relative, but if it's true, it's much longer than what the ledger says." She pointed at the large book on the desk next to the lamp.

*The ledger is real, but not the flashlight?*

"Okay, well, so what? What does it mean?"

Alyssa looked annoyed at his reaction. "So what? You're the one who wanted to investigate this guy. Isn't it odd that he would keep a tally here on the wall of his shower, when he was already keeping a diary out there on paper? I'm thinking he was afraid someone would find his notes."

Joseph shrugged again. "Fair enough, I'll give you that, but still—"

"Also, what do you think this is written in?" She pointed an index finger at the thin, red lines, still looking at Joseph. "See any red permanent markers lying around?"

*Blood.*

Joseph instinctively looked toward the corner of the

fogged-up mirror. There it was again, the line of specks. A constellation of caked blood.

A jarring scream made him jump backward as he turned to Alyssa, her mouth opening wider and wider.

It was happening again. But Alyssa turned into Glenn this time, gaping, and screaming, an endless note of screeching burning in his ears. The figure started stumbling toward him, but Joseph backed out, shut the bathroom door, and bolted out of the room.

The hallway was dark now, like it had been before.

He ran toward the staircase, and in the light from the stairwell he could see the plaque on the wall. He was on the seventh floor again. He decided to run toward what would be his room, hoping Marcia wasn't there.

The sound, the siren song or whatever it was that came from Alyssa-Glenn's mouth was overwhelming. The whole hallway trembled from the vibrations. Joseph removed his hands from his ears and struggled to find his room key. Finally he managed to insert the heavy metal into the lock. It fell into the keyhole, landing securely into its slot.

Joseph flung the door open, splinters flying from the ceiling. Rushing in, he slammed the door behind him. The sound stopped instantly, and Joseph found himself alone, in his room, his bottles of beer scattered about the floor.

*It's true, I drank them all.*

He did nothing but stand for a while, staring down at them. Two lay toppled over on the floor, looking like they might have spilled some leftover beer. The four other ones stood on the side of the desk. The bathroom door was open, and Joseph turned his head slowly to look in at the sink. He needed to check, to know if he'd been in here before with Alyssa, or if this was the first time he had returned this evening.

Lifting himself on his toes, he arched his neck to see inside. He didn't dare step into the bathroom, he didn't want to move. The razor blade was in the same spot: on its side in the sink.

Leaning forward around the wall, looking down the length of his bed, his eyes stopped at the sight of the nightstand. A square paper lay there, frayed at the edges, upside down, exactly how he'd left it.

His head threatened to burst. He was so confused with what was going on. Which days and what events were real? How long had he been here?

His hand found the wound on arm, grabbing at it, wanting to stop his thoughts from racing. Joseph's feet wanted to walk around the end of the bed so he could grab the photograph of Mel, but his hands wanted to snatch the razor blade from the bathroom sink.

His mind refused to let him step into the bathroom, so his body compromised, grabbing a fresh razor blade from the lid of his suitcase before he stepped up to the bed, sat down and grabbed the photograph. He turned it over in his left hand while he unbuttoned the shirt around his wrist, rolled it up, and stopped to stare. Fresh, red blood began to ooze from underneath the dark crust.

"Mel," he whispered, dragging his fingers softly over her face in the photograph. "What's happening to me?"

Joseph looked down at his arm. *Should I finally do it? One last cut, a bit farther down, would be all it takes. I can lie here on the bed, Mel in my arms, all these nightmares out of my head.*

His right hand trembled, clenching the razor blade. Again, his hands wanted to do the one thing they were getting so good at, eager to cut across the saggy flesh of his lower arm, but his mind wouldn't let them. They were fighting, a tug of war between intellect and limbs, Joseph stuck in the middle. One second, two seconds, three. He cut a larger and longer gash next to his latest wound. There was a delay in his body's reaction before the blood started rolling, thundering down his arm as relief flowed through him. It felt like removing a noose, like stepping out into fresh air.

"Maybe this one will do," he said to himself, not sure if he was hoping or asking.

He fell back onto the bed with the picture of Mel gripped tight to his chest. Warmth radiated from his sticky arm. He would deal with it when he woke up.

*If I wake up.*

All he wanted was to sleep, to forget, and not feel so burdened anymore. All he wanted was peace.

J oseph rubbed the sleep out of his eyes as he stepped out into the lobby.

"Ah, Mr. Podwall. Sleep well, sir?" Bryan greeted him with his unconvincing grin. "Too late for breakfast I'm afraid, but just in time for lunch, if you care to join us?"

Joseph ignored the man with the obviously fake enthusiasm. "Is there a phone I can borrow?"

"Certainly, sir." For a second, Joseph hoped he would be led into the back office where he thought he'd overheard someone on the phone the other day, but Bryan promptly lifted a telephone up from under the reception desk. "Take however long you need, no charge." The boy smiled.

Joseph didn't hesitate. Not knowing who to call, only that he needed to speak with someone, he dialed the first number he could remember.

Susan.

As soon as he heard it ring, so did the phone in the back office. He let it ring twice before hanging up. As soon as he did, the echoing ring stopped as well. Not wanting to believe it, he carefully dialed again.

Joseph didn't even raise the receiver to his ear. After a few seconds, the phone rang from the back office again, and Joseph slammed the receiver down.

"Lunch, sir?" Bryan didn't seem fazed by the ringing phone, holding his hand out to welcome Joseph into the dining room, and Joseph wasn't about to resist. He was too disturbed by everything that was going on.

As he walked into the lounge, Joseph tried to remember *when* he had gotten out of bed. Getting in was clear in his memory—picture of Mel, cut on his arm—but when did he get up? His arm didn't hurt either. His blue shirt was rolled down and buttoned up properly. Tapping it gently, it didn't feel like there was a large, fresh cut there. Just the other cut, the smaller one, from the first day.

The dining room was back to its normal layout, rectangular tables, white tableclothes.

*If this is the same lunch all over again, I don't know what I'll do.*

Alyssa was sitting in their usual spot at end of the room. He could see she expected him to come join her. He took a second to scan the room first, looking for who else—or what else—was there.

Glenn sat alone, like he did every time he'd been there. The two guys in the bar were drinking coffee, staring out in front of them. Clyde and Marcia sat where they were supposed to be—Clyde facing out toward the room like he had the last time, but not staring at Joseph.

The young father and his daughter—the couple Clyde said were Joseph and Mel—weren't there. Neither was the young mother and the kid who'd been there the first time. After another quick glance around the room, Joseph went to take his seat by Alyssa.

*It's all the same, but different.*

"Morning," Joseph said, sitting down as Bryan came over to serve them. Roast this time, not soup.

"Morning?" Alyssa laughed. "This is lunch, I'll have you know. Do you always sleep this late?"

"I don't make a habit of it, no," Joseph said, trying to

change the subject. "Remind me, how many times have we had lunch together?"

Alyssa gave a confused frown. "Only once, yesterday. Was I that bad a company that you've forgotten?" She giggled, cutting into her meal.

"No, I . . . Just a bit confused is all."

"You disappeared quickly last night," Alyssa said.

"What?" Joseph blurted in the middle of biting over his fork. *That really happened then?*

"From Doru's room. You left after we discussed the markings in the shower. The tally marks."

*So it* did *happen.*

"I—I can't remember. I probably had too much to drink. Did I say anything before I left?"

Alyssa frowned. "No, you just . . . left. Without a word, really. One minute we were in the bathroom, discussing those red marks on the wall. I mentioned they might be blood, and then you left. I figured it was the alcohol—again."

"Yeah." Joseph didn't understand. "Must have been."

"Sleep well?"

Joseph looked down at his forearm, shirt buttoned over it. He gave it a casual squeeze as he thought about Alyssa's question and felt a searing pain. *The cut is definitely there.*

"Yeah, as well as I could have," he said without looking up.

He was finally starting to get a grasp of what was real and not. This was real—him and Alyssa, going to room 532. Not the courtyard and talking to Clyde and Marcia.

Thinking about the detectives, Joseph cast them a glance over his glass of water. Clyde already finished his roast and was enjoying his coffee and raised his cup slightly and nodded in his direction.

*Do they know me? Have I actually talked to them or not?*

"Did we talk to the two police detectives yesterday?"

Alyssa hummed, chewing and swallowing before she was ready to answer.

"Who? Those two?" She threw her head toward the men at the bar.

Joseph shook his head slowly. "No, those two." He pointed with his ring finger, still holding his glass. "The man in the coat and the woman."

"Who told you they're police?"

"You did," he said, trying his best not to raise his voice.

"No, I didn't. I have no idea who they are. I know someone's been saying that those two at the bar *might* be police, but I don't know about the man in the trench coat."

Joseph's hand trembled, the glass shaking. This was getting ridiculous. He gently set down his drink, placing his hand on the table, hoping that Alyssa wouldn't notice.

"Okay, fine," he said. "Those two men then. We haven't talked to them, have we?"

"I haven't." Alyssa shrugged. "I can't know what you have or haven't done." She carried on eating, tiny bites at a time.

"And what about the man in the coat and the woman—regardless of who they are—did we talk to them?"

"No, I've . . ." She put her knife and fork down. "You're being weird, Joseph. This looking into Doru's disappearance has really gotten to you, hasn't it?"

"You didn't answer my question."

She met his eyes with an intense stare. "And you avoided mine."

"Answer mine first. Did we speak to those two, yesterday? When we had lunch, did I get up, go over there, and talk to them?"

"Not that I recall, no. We sat here enjoying the soup before I went back to work and you went upstairs. We didn't meet again until last night, so I don't know what you did."

She placed a gentle hand on top of his but then pulled back quickly. Her delicate fingers stilled next to his on the table. "Joseph, what's going on?"

"I'm . . . Do you believe in the supernatural?"

She withdrew a bit, sitting straighter. "Like, ghosts and stuff?"

"Maybe, but at the same time, not ghosts and stuff. Things that are impossible. Weird things."

"I don't know. Why? Are you talking about the hotel again?" She picked up her knife and fork.

"I've had . . . experiences. Events layered between events, and I'm not sure what's real or not."

"Are you sure you're not having night terrors? This place is old. It creaks and moans in the wind, that takes some time getting used to."

Joseph sighed, scratching his stubble. "We were in the courtyard, yesterday. Clyde"—he pointed across the room—"interrogated me, under suspicion of your disappearance. *Yours*, Alyssa. You'd been missing for five days. According to Clyde, I'd been here for a week. But I checked in yesterday, didn't I?"

Alyssa's face tried to appear gleeful, her default social operating mode, but her eyes and mouth were wrought with worry. "We weren't in the—"

"*But we were.* This is what I mean. I've had entire series of events happening, together with you, that aren't real—or so it seems. We were outside in the courtyard, looking for the photograph of my daughter, which I'd lost out the window in Doru's room."

"Why would your photograph be there? You never lost anything out that window. We didn't even open it."

Joseph slammed a clenched fist on the table. "But it happened! When we entered his room, that room was my room. I know it doesn't make sense. Which is why I asked you—do you believe in the supernatural?"

"I—I'm not sure."

"But according to you, none of this happened?"

"No, of course not, Joseph. We had lunch and went to Doru's room, and that was last night."

"Do you still have the ledger?"

"I put it back in the reception last night, why?"

Joseph looked out through to the lobby. He couldn't see the pasty teenager standing behind the desk, so maybe he could sneak a peek later. "Don't worry about it." He picked his napkin out of his lap and folded it neatly on top of the table. "I'm not hungry. I think I'll head back to my room."

Alyssa didn't say anything, but when he pushed his chair back to stand, she said, "Wait."

Joseph sat back down, waiting for what she was looking for. Alyssa grabbed her purse off the floor and pulled a piece of paper out of her purse. "I'm not sure what to believe, but I found this after you left yesterday."

At first, Joseph thought it was his photograph of him and Mel, but as she put it down in front of him, he recognized it as one of the notes they'd found in Doru's room. One of his diary entries.

"What do you want me to do with this?" Joseph asked.

"Read it."

Joseph scanned it over. It didn't say much. Ramblings, some indecipherable writing. The little he could actually read was about a man named Doru, about his stay, how he hated it, loved it, and didn't belong.

"I don't see what this is supposed to say," Joseph began.

"Remember last night, we found a few of these." Alyssa leaned an elbow on the table, her other hand gesturing at the note. "I've read them all. Remember how I said he'd written detailed experiences about meeting me, talking to me, and so on? Which is kind of odd, because I don't really recall him. Then again, there can be a lot of people coming through here."

*I find that hard to believe.* "Yeah, and?"

Alyssa pointed to the bottom of the page, most of which Joseph couldn't read due to Doru's difficult handwriting. Joseph looked closer and saw it spelled out right in front of him.

*Met Joe today. He's not like everyone else in here. I like him.*

"What does the rest say?"

Joseph took the note from her and looked at it closer.

*Joseph came to my room today. He's nice. Not like the others. He's different.*

Alyssa looked up at Joseph again. "Doru's met you too, it sounds like. You've been to his room."

"That's impossible. He disappeared before I even checked in."

Alyssa cleared her throat, casting a quick glance down at the paper. "Because you definitely checked in yesterday?"

"If you're questioning that as well, then it sounds like you're starting to believe me?"

"After reading this, I—I don't know what to believe."

Joseph rose from his seat in a hurry. "I've had enough of

this." Heads turned as he pushed his chair to the floor, but he didn't care. Striding straight out into the lobby, he stepped over to the reception desk, leaned over and grabbed the big, leather-bound tome that was the guest ledger.

Bryan came rushing out of the back room.

"Sir, what are you doing?" Bryan went to grab the book, but Joseph turned around, leaning on the desk with his back to Bryan, flipping casually through the pages of the book.

"Don't mind me, Bry," he said.

Bryan grabbed at Joseph's shoulders. "You can't have that, it's the hotel's property!" Bryan's voice sounded frantic. His arms were outstretched, hands flailing over the reception desk but he was unable to reach the book.

"I know, I know. It will just take a minute. You'll have your precious book back soon enough."

Joseph found the entry for Doru Amani a few pages in. He'd been there for a while and never checked out—just like Joseph and Alyssa had concluded the other night. Room 532 was also correct. Joseph looked over the note again, making sure he hadn't misread, before he flipped toward today's date to find his own entry. Blinking forcefully, he had to shake his head and read the line over and over again, when he saw that—according to the ledger—Joseph Podwall had been at the hotel for seven days.

"What the fuck is this?" Joseph turned to Bryan, slamming the book down on the counter. He spun it around toward Bryan, pointing at his own entry. "When did I check in?"

Bryan latched onto the edges of the book.

"Y—you . . . you checked in a-a-a week ago. T-today." His jaw clenched, and he violently pulled the book out of Joseph's grasp, placing it underneath the desk where it was supposed to be. Straightening himself and combing his hair into place with one hand, he was much more his normal self. "Now, if there's anything else I can do for you, Mr. Podwall, please do not hesitate to ask."

Joseph pointed a thick finger at Bryan's face. "Bullshit. I didn't check in a week ago. I checked in yesterday."

The boy wasn't deterred. "I'm sorry to say you're mistaken, Mr. Podwall. Now, I have other matters to attend to." Bryan left to go back into the office behind the desk.

"Who's in there with you?" Joseph yelled. "Who's the person who doesn't want to come out?"

Stepping back into the doorway, looking at Joseph first, and then back into the small room, Bryan grew a confused frown. "There's no one else here but me, I assure you, Mr. Podwall."

"Fuck you, there's not."

Joseph stepped around the desk, pushing past the slender teenager and into the back room. Bryan's hands grabbed for him, trying to stop him from entering his little sanctuary, but it was no use. Joseph pushed past him with ease.

It was a small room, not more than eight feet across. A worn-out couch lined the far corner, stretching out further on one wall than the other. A low, round table stood in front of it, with empty beer bottles, dirty coffee mugs, and overflowing ashtrays. An old TV set stood against the wall facing out into the lobby, but the TV wasn't even plugged in. Some of the wires were bare, looking like they had been stripped. A few books were piled up on the end of the couch, and the whole room was lit with a single, buzzing light bulb.

"What do you want?" Bryan yelled, pushing in front of Joseph again, taking a defensive stance in the middle of the room. "There's no one here, it's—it's just me here. It's my room."

Joseph was dumbstruck. "You live like this?"

Bryan pushed at Joseph's chest in frustration. "Why do you

care?"

It didn't do much to push him back, but Joseph took the hint, and stepped back out into the lobby.

"I apologize," he said as he stepped toward the dining lounge. He was sure he had heard someone in there, shuffling around. He could swear he had heard Bryan talk to them. *Maybe he talks to himself.*

At least he'd figured out the truth, if he could believe the guest book. Joseph had been there longer than he thought.

"Alyssa?" Joseph asked as he rounded the corner into the dining lounge, but to his surprise, she was gone. Finished her lunch and left, Joseph figured. As had Glenn, and Clyde and Marcia. Even their plates were gone, but who had taken them? Joseph had been with Bryan since he'd left the table, and he hadn't seen anyone else work in the lounge.

The two men at the bar were still there though, the men who, according to Alyssa—this time around at least—were the police detectives, not Clyde and Marcia.

*It's not like this isn't weird enough as it is.*

Joseph walked over to introduce himself. They both turned to him simultaneously, one hopping a stool to the right, making room for Joseph in the middle.

"Come, Joe. Have a seat," the one on the left said. "We have much to talk about."

Neither their behavior nor the fact that they knew his name surprised Joseph at all. Nothing did anymore.

The one on the left held out a hand. Joseph took it and shook. "They call me Baker."

Baker had a short crown of black hair around his head, balding on top. He was a chunk of man, with underarms bigger than Joseph's biceps and a sagging double chin.

The man on the right introduced himself as Carver.

His hair and beard were red, receding in the front. He was

much more slender than his partner, taller as well, though it was difficult to tell when they were sitting down. They were both smoking, and a coffee cup sat in front of each of them.

*Baker and Carver, huh? What is this, a farmer's market?*

"Pleasure to meet you both," Joseph said after shaking their hands, not sure who to address first. "What is it we have to talk about?" he asked Baker.

Baker stumped his cigarette, grabbed another one out of the chest pocket of his dirty, washed-out shirt. He lit his smoke while still exhaling smoke from the previous one.

"Smoke?" Baker asked, but Joseph shook his head, and Baker didn't press. "We need to talk about The Gate." He motioned to the room. "This place. By now I'm sure you've noticed what it's doing to all of us."

Joseph's stare glided between the two of them, Baker on the left, Carver on the right, before he decided to settle on the mirror in front of them. He understood why they'd been sitting like this, staring out into nothing, because from here he could see both of them.

"Actually, I'll take that cigarette," he said to Baker, who withdrew one from his shirt pocket and pushed the box of matches along the bar, together with the ashtray.

Joseph lit the cigarette, taking a deep, nauseating drag. He held it for a second or three, finally letting out a slow billow of smoke. "Yes, I've . . . noticed things. What do you two know about it?"

"What did the woman say about us?" Carver asked in a hoarse, thin voice. "The pretty one, during lunch. We saw you talking about us."

"Alyssa? She said you two were cops. Investigating the disappearance of Doru Amani."

Both Carver and Baker burst out in laughter. Carver sounded like a maniac clown with his high-pitched whistling, while Baker sounded like a steam engine, his laughter rolling out in waves.

"She said *we* were the cops?" Baker asked in a rumbling voice.

"Yeah, I actually thought Clyde and Marcia, the couple who sits over—" Joseph turned to point at their usual table, but Baker put a hand on his shoulder, keeping him from spinning around.

"Listen, none of them are cops. We're not cops, they're not cops. The girl, Alyssa, she's not what she seems."

Joseph craned his neck backward. "What's that supposed to mean?"

"I'm going to take a wild stab here, and say that you've experienced some pretty fucked up shit in here, haven't you?" Baker took a long drag off his smoke.

Looking at them both in the mirror behind the bar, Joseph saw they were both staring at him, hard. "Yeah," he answered hesitantly.

"And I'll bet Alyssa—the little dove—is at the center of all of it, isn't she? In addition to yourself, of course."

Joseph hadn't thought about it before, because Bryan had also been there, as well as Glenn, Clyde, and Marcia. But Alyssa was the only one who'd been there for all of it—or at least been instrumental to all of it.

"Yeah, she is."

"She said she works in the bar, didn't she? Pouring us all drinks, keeping us all satisfied and out of the way."

Joseph nodded carefully, looking at the bar in front of all of them.

"And how many times have you seen her work here?"

"She made me a cocktail when I first checked in."

"Yeah, she does that," Carver said. "And since then, she's never been back."

"Okay, I'm convinced," Joseph said with another puff of his cigarette. "But what does that mean? Who is she then?"

"We don't know. But we think she runs this place, together with Bryan maybe, but he seems more clueless than anything. We also think Doru knows more than he lets on, but we haven't seen him in a while."

"He's missing, isn't he?"

"Hah!" Baker grunted. "She told you that too, didn't she?"

*She did, in fact.* "Yeah, and she—"

"Asked you to help her find him?" Carver said, a knowing glint in his eye.

"Yeah, that's what she told us. Doru isn't missing." Baker smiled. "He's hiding." He finished his coffee then twisted on top of his stool. "We tried to help her at first, until everything went weird. Rooms changing, time missing. You've noticed it too, right?"

"Yes. "Joseph nodded along. "More than I care to admit."

"How's the arm?" Baker asked. Joseph didn't quite understand what he meant until he saw Baker staring at the shirt over his forearm. "How many is it now? Two, or three?"

Joseph put a protective hand over his left arm. "How do you know about that?"

"I'm not sure. There's a lot of things we know, and very few explanations for how we know them. Ain't that right, Carver?"

Joseph looked at Carver in the mirror, who nodded. His crooked nose looked like it had been broken a few times.

Baker pulled another cigarette out of his shirt pocket and handed it to Joseph, who hadn't realized he had finished his first.

"How do you think we knew your name, Joe?"

Joseph was about to interrupt with his usual line, but Baker beat him to it.

"Yeah, yeah, we know that too. Your name's Joseph. Fine.

Whatever you say."

Baker lit yet another cigarette and took a nice long drag. Joseph was confused about whether they had more to say or if they expected him to speak. The silence was becoming awkward before Baker eventually spoke up.

"Listen, Joseph. Me and Carver have been figuring out quite a bit, but frankly, I think we're both too stupid to figure out the rest. But we know two things for certain. This bar, this place right here, is safe. That's why we're always sitting here. Everywhere else, you're fucked. You can't trust what's real, what's really happening, or anything. Believe me, we haven't left our seats in, how long?" He looked over at Carver who squinted up at the ceiling, counting on his fingers.

"I don't know, nine, ten days?"

"There you go, Joe. Ten days, we've sat here, we've drunk coffee and smoked. Haven't even had a piss, no less a shit, or a night of sleep or anything."

"If that's true—and I'm not saying it is, because that sounds insane—then it sounds like this isn't a safe place? It sounds like this place is just as fucked up as the rest of the hotel. If this was normal, you wouldn't have survived sitting here like that."

Baker shrugged and pursed his lips. "Yeah, maybe. I hadn't thought of it like that. But at least, here, we're left in peace. No weird bullshit, no lost time, no crazy nothing. That's a plus in my book at least."

"What's the other thing? The other thing you know." Joseph's hand was trembling again, so he interlaced his fingers together and settled them on the bar.

"Oh right." Baker turned to stare directly at Joseph. "We know where Doru is. For me and Carver, it's safe to sit here because Alyssa doesn't care about us anymore. But Doru—I don't know man, she's looking for Doru. He told me where he's hiding. Now, I get it, you're probably going to talk to Alyssa after this. You're going to tell her everything we said."

"No, I wouldn't—" Joseph lied.

"It's okay, we don't care, tell her whatever you want. But that's on you, okay?"

Joseph raised an eyebrow, but Baker didn't elaborate. "Sure, I'll keep that in mind . . ."

Baker looked past Joseph, and Joseph saw the two men share a glance past his head. "Okay. Doru is hiding upstairs. He's on your floor. In room 708."

The room number rang a bell in Joseph's head, but it took him a few seconds before he remembered why. "Are you sure that's the one? I don't think—"

"It's that one, definitely. 708. Go up there, say you've talked to Baker. Doru will open."

Baker and Carver turned around to continue smoking, drinking, and staring at each other in the mirror. Joseph sensed the conversation was over and slid off the stool. Carver was quick to take back his seat next to Baker. Joseph wandered slowly out of the dining lounge, still empty except for Baker and Carver.

Bryan stood behind his desk in the reception, looking up at him with a bright smile as if nothing had happened earlier, as if Joseph had never wrestled his way into Bryan's little nest, or stolen his ledger out from underneath the desk.

"Afternoon, sir."

"Afternoon," Joseph replied, squinting at the boy as he passed. *What are you up to?*

As soon as Joseph put his foot on the first step in the staircase, the elevator reminded him of its broken existence by powering up its whirring and clanking. *Yeah, yeah. I know you're there.*

He stomped up the stairs and stopped to push the call

button for the elevator on every floor. If he couldn't use the elevator, then he was going to be sure as hell no one else could either.

Stopping on the fifth floor for a breather, winded as usual, Joseph stared at the door leading through to the hallway. He wanted to go back there. Back to room 532 to look for Doru in his alleged old room instead of going up to 708.

*There was only a child and a woman up there, the ones from the first lunch, I'm guessing. Are they hiding Doru?*

Joseph stared at the door to the fifth floor once more before taking a deep breath and carrying on up the stairs. Finally on the seventh floor, he double-checked the plaque indicating where the rooms were and took a right.

Joseph walked on autopilot. The talk with Baker and Carver had numbed him. They'd stripped away all of what he thought was reality and replaced it with something else.

He would have to talk to Alyssa later, of course, and as Baker predicted, Joseph would probably tell her what they'd said. He wasn't sure who he was more inclined to believe.

But they had a point. She was at the center of everything, in one way or another. And it didn't feel like they were lying to him, but if they were, he couldn't see what their agenda would be. What were they gaining from pitting him against Alyssa?

As he stopped outside his room, he wondered if they were sending him into a trap. There was no evidence that Doru would be in there. It could be an attempt to get rid of him, but he needed answers.

He slipped into his room to grab a fresh razor blade from his suitcase and dropped it in his pocket. Not much of a weapon, but the only thing he had so it had to be good enough.

*If I can cut myself with it, it sure as hell can cut someone else.*

Locking his door behind him, he continued down the hallway.

Assuming it was a trap set up by Baker and Carver, what could he expect? There was no way they could have beat him up here, but then again, both his luggage and his order of beers had managed to sneak past him. They could be waiting in the room for him, but to do what? They didn't seem particularly hostile downstairs, and Alyssa even claimed they were detectives. Which was another thing that didn't fit into the puzzle. If Alyssa wasn't who she seemed, she would surely have known that Baker and Carver weren't cops. What did she gain by lying and saying they were?

Joseph rubbed a hand across his face as he tried to make sense of it. One of the parties were lying, but who?

Turning to the side, Joseph saw that the door he was facing was room 712. *What?*

He whirled around, uncertain of how he could have passed 708. *Was I that lost in my thoughts?*

He spun around again, only to stop and stare at the door again, taking an unsure step backward. It read 708.

*It literally just said 712, what the fuck?*

He closed and opened his eyes. It was still 708. Lifting his hand toward the door, he half expected it to disappear or come flying at him or do something unimaginable. But it remained a silent, inanimate door.

He knocked. Again, and again. Nothing happened. No one opened, no one answered. Just as Joseph was about to knock again, he heard crying from inside the room and a sense of déjà vu washed over him. The crying sounded like that of a child, an infant, wailing for food, a mother, a warm touch.

"Doru?" he called out instinctively, not sure why he thought that was the right thing to ask, but the crying seized. Joseph thought he could hear movement. After a few seconds, he asked again, "Doru?" and then the lock of the door clicked, the door slowly swinging open.

There was a little boy, six, maybe seven years old in the doorway.

"Hi," Joseph said carefully. "Are you okay?"

"Hi, Joe," the boy opened the door wide. "Come in. I've been waiting for you."

Joseph hesitated, contemplating the boy for a moment before he walked into the small room. It was identical to his, but better lit because there was an extra lamp on the nightstand. The blonde woman from lunch the other day was sitting on the bed, staring out the window.

"Hello," Joseph said nervously, giving her an awkward wave. She didn't seem to notice, or care, and kept staring out the window. The boy came up to them, sat down on the foot of the bed, and motioned for Joseph to take the chair by the desk.

"Is that your mother?" Joseph asked, slightly nervous as to why the grown woman wasn't acknowledging them.

"You can cut it out, Joe, she's not real," the boy said, snapping his fingers. The woman disappeared, shimmering away. It startled Joseph so severely that he jolted into the desk behind him.

"What the flying fuck was that?" he screamed at the boy.

"I'm sorry, Joe, I thought you knew as much by now. That you've understood who I am?"

Joseph had considered it, of course. The boy was the only one in the room, but he hadn't dared to think it could be true.

"I'm Doru," the boy finished.

Joseph stared at the boy in disbelief. Here he was, the missing guest. A child. "Of course you are," Joseph muttered. He pointed to the spot on the bed where the woman had been sitting. "How'd you do that?"

"You can do a lot of things in here when you know the rules," Doru gestured at himself. "I don't suppose you think I'm a—"

"A child?" Joseph said. "No, but it's a hell of a good disguise. And that . . ." Joseph pointed to the spot on the bed again as he struggled to find the word. "Illusion? She was your cover? Your mother?"

"Yup."

"Well done," Joseph said while looking for more words to describe his confusion. When he realized he couldn't find any, he shook the thought out of his head. "Well done." He took a second to look around the room again. It was the same as his, other than the extra lamp, and Doru's room didn't have Joseph's suitcase. "So, why are you hiding, and why have I come to find you? I assume you know that Baker sent me?"

"Yes. And you know why I'm hiding. I'm hiding from her."

"Alyssa?"

"Yes."

"Why? What's Alyssa want with you that's so bad?"

"She wants me to stay. She wants us all to stay." Doru still held the appearance of a child but spoke with the confidence and composure of a grown man.

"And you don't want to stay?"

"Let me ask you something, Joseph," Doru said, repositioning his small body on the bed. "Three questions." He held up his little hand with three fingers raised, ready to count down. "How long have you been here, how long do you *think* you've been here, and how long do you plan on staying?"

Joseph knew the answers to the first two. According to the ledger he'd been there a week, even though he only remembered the first two days. He didn't know which one of those two were real, but going by Doru's questioning, he could guess.

The last question was difficult to answer. When he checked in, he didn't really have a time he needed to leave. It was another hotel, another . . . week? Or weekend? He just wanted some time away, for himself, to drink, and . . . He rubbed his arm casually.

Doru nodded toward Joseph's arm. "You don't know when you planned on leaving, did you? Because you didn't plan on walking out yourself?"

"Maybe. So what?"

"Frank brought you here, right?"

Joseph nodded.

"Yeah, Frank brings everyone here. Do you remember where he picked you up? When you called him to come get you?"

As Joseph thought about it, his face must have given him away.

"No, no one ever does. Me, Baker, Carver, even Glenn, if you believe it, were brought here by Frank. Maybe Bryan as well, but I never found the time to ask. Clyde and Marcia—" Doru cocked his head, his eyes staring off into the corner. "I'm not so sure. They seem to be in Alyssa's court."

"Yeah, but I booked a stay. Frank might have picked me up, but it's not like I wasn't coming here anyway."

"Are you sure about that?" Doru sighed. "You tried calling someone, didn't you? But the number you dialed was to the hotel."

"How did you know that?"

"I know a lot of things, Joseph." They stared at each other for a while, a sense of dread in the boy's eyes reached Joseph.

"What's the point of this place then? Why does Alyssa keep us here?" Joseph asked.

"Hell?" Doru asked in a voice that suggested he might mean it. Joseph looked confused for a second, before Doru started laughing. "No, that's something Carver said. He said this place is hell, but I don't think so. In any case, I'd say it's limbo."

*That would explain all the weird shit that's going on here.*

Joseph looked around the room as if it would shift into another dimension when its truth was finally revealed.

"I think Alyssa wants different things from each of us. Whatever she is, or this is." Doru gestured at the room, at the hotel. "She says she wants to help us. That's what she told me, at least. What has she said to you?"

*What has she said to me?*

"She wanted me to help find you. Because you'd disappeared, gone missing. I'm a travel writer. I love when a place has a good mystery. Sounded like a fun thing to do before I . . . before I checked out, so of course I wanted to help her. Hook, line, and sinker, I fell for all of it. And here you are, locked away inside this room. But I'm not sure what else she said."

"Travel writer sounds like an interesting job," Doru said. "You must see a lot of places."

Joseph nodded, lowering his head toward the carpet, thinking hard about what Alyssa had wanted from him specifically. Then his eyes searched for the window and remained there, locked on the darkness outside.

"My daughter," Joseph said. "She showed an interest in her, and wanted to help me find a photograph, to find my daughter."

"Is your daughter here?"

"No, no she's dead. I only have the photograph."

"Sounds strange. I don't see what she'd get out of that," Doru mused.

"What did you mean when you said she wanted to help you? Help you with what?"

Doru's eyes became glassy, thoughtful. "She said she'd help me get out of here. Escape. We'd meet in the bar regularly for lunch."

Joseph huffed. *Sounds familiar.*

"But everything we did worked against me. We never made any plans to leave, there was always another meeting. She kept saying I had to stay, had to wait. That's when I realized she'd never let me leave. There was always one more day. So, I started prying. Talked with Clyde and Marcia. They seemed understanding at first, but not like they shared my worries. Bryan didn't either, but you've met him. He's strange, at best. Then I met Baker and Carver. Can't remember exactly what they said, but they told me they'd been here for ages. Trying to get out at first. Sitting at the bar later." Doru stared down at his hands. "Then I realized I could change. You can change too, can't you?"

Looking at his own hands, Joseph only saw the sad reality of how old he was. He flexed his fingers, watching the veins and tendons dance. The same old hands he'd always had, but he looked younger the other day. "Yeah, I think so. I'm not sure how though."

"Hmm." Doru flipped his hands back and forth. "I can change. Myself, things around me. Alyssa didn't recognize me like this, so this is what I became. I conjured my mother to stay with me. Less suspicious. She's still searching for me, but so far, I think I'm safe."

"Maybe you were the one who changed me then?" Joseph suggested. "The other day, I was younger. My daughter, Mel, was there as well. It freaked me out."

Doru's eyes grew wide. "Mel's your daughter? The girl?"

Joseph was slightly taken aback by his reaction. "Yes, why?"

"Because I've seen her too. She lives here. She can't be dead, she's a guest."

"What?" Joseph threw himself out of his seat. Doru recoiled onto the bed as Joseph stalked forward. "Where is she?"

"I—I don't know. I thought she was just another guest. Last I saw of her, she was playing in the courtyard. Earlier today."

Joseph stormed out the door. He flew down the hall toward the stairwell and heard the elevator ding. It made him stop in his tracks even though he was certain it was a trick. Was it working? Was it on the seventh floor now? Would it open if he pressed the call button? If there ever was a trap laid out right in front of him, it was this. Joseph took the stairs.

He could see Bryan's mouth begin to open as he rounded the bottom of the stairs—if Bryan even had a mouth or even was a person.

"Fuck off, Bryan!" he said as he rushed through the lobby.

The tall, wide hall leading to the courtyard wasn't the same as before. It was white this time. *Here we go, another trick.*

Joseph spun around as he walked, taking in his surroundings. White and bland, almost medical. A few lights on the walls, like before, and a slick tiled floor. Nothing remarkable about it, nothing to remember it by.

He burst through the double doors at the end into the large room again, the ballroom. It looked the same, but large round tables were set up for guests. Plate, cutlery, and glass at every seat. Black napkins. It looked dreary, depressing, and eerily familiar.

Turning the corner, he came upon the heavy wooden doors Alyssa had struggled to open. The ones that led outside. Joseph could only hope they were still unlocked. If he and Alyssa hadn't actually been out there, would they be? Pushing a shoulder against the double doors, they slowly creaked open.

"Mel?" he shouted into a gust of wind. No, not a gust. A full-on thunderstorm. Lightning cracked across the sky, tearing open the clouds as it started to pour.

Joseph shielded his face, the wind and rain whipping at him violently. He heard laughter. A child's laughter.

"Mel! Where are you?" Joseph struggled to even move against the force of the storm. The bushes on the edge of the circular courtyard lay flat against the concrete.

"Mel? Sweetie?" Joseph didn't know if he was calling a little girl or a grown woman. She had been nineteen when she died, but he didn't know if that was who she was here. Doru described her as a little girl, after all. Joseph supposed that with all the other ridiculous things happening, his daughter being alive again would not be the strangest.

Struggling against the wind, making his way toward the fountain in the middle, he began to realize she couldn't be there. All the bushes were lying flat in the wind. There was nowhere left to hide.

And that was when he saw it, as he lumbered toward the fountain. Except it wasn't a fountain anymore. It was a gravestone.

*Here Lies*

*Melanie*

*Our Little Sweetheart*

JOSEPH'S BREATH CAUGHT. His heart beat so slowly he wasn't sure if it was even beating at all. The courtyard around him wasn't a courtyard anymore, it was the secluded meadow where they had buried her, all those years ago. The double doors still stood in either end, opposite each other, with nothing but on the other sides, just forest as far as he could see.

*What is this?*

Tears poured from his eyes. Regret bubbled up inside his chest, followed by anger, quick to wash away anything that could even resemble sadness.

Looking back at the double doors behind him, he was reminded of where he had come from—that terrifying, confusing hotel—and he wasn't about to go back that way.

He needed to move forward.

Dragging his feet, heavy like logs underneath him, he began to lumber toward the other set of doors. Locked or not, Joseph was intent on giving it a try. The force of 250 pounds of aging man, moving at whatever measly speed Joseph could produce was apparently enough to do the trick. The doors sprang open, and Joseph fell in—right into the lobby, onto the floor in front of Bryan.

"Good evening, sir." Bryan smiled.

Joseph pushed himself to his feet and noticed his clothes were completely dry—except for where his tears had stained his shirt.

He wanted to continue being angry, to be upset with the madness, but sorrow and exhaustion were all that was left. He was so tired, tired of this game.

*I should have ended it all when I arrived. I wouldn't have had to relive this—wouldn't have to face this pain once more.*

He looked back at the doors he had come through—the doors that should have gone out to the street—and couldn't even begin to try and wrap his head around what just happened.

"Good evening, Bryan," he said instead, pushing himself off the floor and starting the arduous walk upstairs. The courtyard was Mel's graveyard, and suddenly he understood why the large hallway had been white. It was the morgue where he and his wife had waited. The familiar ballroom was where they had gathered afterward to put Mel to rest.

*Carver was right. This is hell.*

Joseph unbuttoned his shirt. By the time he was standing outside the door to his room, he had taken the shirt all the way off, revealing his white undershirt.

*This is hell, and I might as well be dead.*

Doru would probably still be where he was, hiding away, in the guise of the child in 708. Joseph could go over there, get more answers, perhaps. But it had been too much.

*Unless I already am dead.*

Seeing Mel's grave, hearing her laugh, it was too much. It was so painful living without her. So exhausting. He just wanted to sleep. Stepping through the door to his room, he grabbed a razor blade from his suitcase and slid the blade down both arms.

J oseph remembered hearing Clyde's voice for some reason. Clyde and Marcia were there, but he wasn't sure where he was—was it in his room?

They were talking to each other, and Joseph was . . .

*Am I lying on the floor? Is this it, am I dead? If death is lying in a dark room with Clyde and Marcia, I'd rather suffer through another few years of life.*

It felt like he was on his bed, and they were standing over him. They'd probably come to interrogate him again, and carried him to bed. Clyde's heavy hands were on top of Joseph. He could feel them, like they were reassuring Clyde that Joseph was still there, was still alive.

*Why can't I see? Why is it so dark?*

His body ached as if he'd been lying there for hours on end. He tried to force himself awake, tried to listen in on the conversation around him.

And when he finally managed to open his eyes, it wasn't Clyde who was there. Instead, Joseph stared right into the face of Alyssa. He wasn't lying on his bed anymore, but sitting upright, in the lounge. Alyssa was in the chair next to him, chewing what presumably was breakfast.

He saw the young boy and the woman, Doru and his illusion; Clyde and Marcia, facing him; Glenn, sitting alone; and Baker and Carver, sitting at the bar. Baker nodded at Joseph and raised his coffee cup.

"Fuck!" Joseph screamed at the top of his lungs. Everyone jumped in their seat.

"Jesus Christ," Alyssa said, dropping her fork onto her plate. "You scared me, Joseph. What's going on?"

"No! Fuck you, Alyssa. You're going to tell *me* what's going on."

His wrists burned like a motherfucker. Rolling up the sleeves of his shirt slightly he saw two large gashes, one on each arm.

*How the hell did I survive that? And how did I end up here at the table?*

"What are you doing to me?"

"What do you mean?" She slowly picked her fork back up and continued eating. Scrambled eggs, ham, and sourdough bread.

"What are you? A demon? Spirit? A malevolent angel?"

"First of all, offensive. Second, no. What's the matter with you?"

"I tried to kill myself last night!" Joseph shouted.

Alyssa shushed him.

"But nothing happened. Look!" He held up the shirt on his right arm showing her the crusty wound. "I don't remember waking up, I don't—"

"Joseph, calm down." Alyssa put her hand on his, pinning it softly to the table. "You shouldn't hurt yourself like that, you need help. Let me help you."

*There it is. The help.*

"Doru said you'd say that."

Her eyes opened wide. "You've found him? Where is he?"

"I'm not going to say," Joseph sneered.

"Why not? He needs my help."

"With what?"

Joseph felt like he saw Doru glare at him from a few tables

over. Maybe he overheard the conversation. But it seemed Doru was right. Alyssa couldn't see through his disguise.

"Please, Joseph. Doru needs my help. As do you. I'll help you leave this place."

"He told me you'd say that too." Joseph leaned back in his chair, crossing his arms. "He said you'd try to help, but there was always another day at The Gate."

"Joseph, you don't understand how it works. Lead me to Doru. Let me explain."

Joseph waved away her words. "If I get up and walk out those doors"—he pointed out toward the street—"can I leave? Will Frank come and pick me up. Because I went to the court-yard earlier, walked through it, and ended up right back here, in the lobby."

"It's not that simple, no." Alyssa looked down into her plate, hesitating. "You can't just leave like that."

"I talked to Baker and Carver yesterday," Joseph said. That got her attention. "Yeah, see, I've been nosing around. They told me you're the one keeping us here. You're the reason we can't leave, and you're not what you seem." Joseph pointed a thick finger in Alyssa's face. "You're the reason Doru is hiding."

Alyssa didn't seem threatened by his accusing hand, only took it between hers, and held it.

"And you know where he is, Joseph. Only you know where Doru is hiding. Please, take me to him."

"Why should I?"

Alyssa leaned closer to him, still holding his large hand in her small ones. "Because Doru is the reason all of us are here," she whispered.

Joseph recoiled, yanking his hand away.

"It's true what Baker and Carver say, in a sense. I'm not like you, I'm not trapped here in the same way. But I'm not evil— I'm not the devil. And I know. I know the cause of this, of all of it. It's . . . it's complicated, but we need to find Doru. Please Joseph, if you know where he's hidden himself away, take me to him. Let me unwind this. Help me help Doru."

Her eyes were pleading. Tiny specks of starlit hope in a dark sky. Joseph couldn't find malice in them, whatever Baker, Carver, or Doru said.

"What about Clyde, and Marcia? Are they stuck here? Are they police like you said earlier? Or are Baker and Carver police like you claimed yesterday?"

A frown formed on her face. "Baker and Carver are not police—no one is. We're not . . ." She lowered her head and sighed. "It's difficult to explain, Joseph. I'm a Watcher. As are Clyde and Marcia, kind of. The rest of you are collateral. You've seen things here, right? Things have happened, like you said about your wrists and waking up here at the table?"

"Yeah?" His wrists burned underneath his shirt.

"And I bet you've seen Doru do things, right? I mean *actually* do things, not just being on the receiving end of it, like you and me."

*She's not wrong.* He had seen Doru make the woman disappear, and she was right there now, having lunch with him less than thirty feet away.

"What if I have?"

"I know you have, and it should prove to you that Doru is the key to all of this. I'm not the one who's not what I seem. He is. Please, let me help him. Take me to him so I can help all of us. He's the one keeping us from leaving, he's the one who changes this place."

Joseph considered it as Alyssa's frown tightened. He didn't dare look over at the child he knew was Doru, but briefly met Baker and Carver's stare in the bar mirror. They both lightly shook their heads.

"What about Glenn?" Joseph asked. "What role does he play in this?"

"Same as you, trapped collateral."

"What about the maid? The old woman?"

"Who?"

He returned the frown, thinking Alyssa was being deliberately obtuse, then he realized he hadn't seen her anywhere else in the hotel. Only in his room.

"There was an old woman, she cleaned my room."

Alyssa's eyebrows raised. "Glenn cleans the rooms, Joseph. I've told you this. Clearly Doru has made you see a great many things. I'll help all of you, as soon as I find him. I need to talk to him, pry him out of hiding. There's so much he doesn't understand."

"He's responsible? For everything? For making my daughter appear in the courtyard, for making me see her grave?" A sadness emerged within him, and rage crept up the back of his neck.

"Joseph." Alyssa leaned in even closer. "Doru is responsible for all of it, and I mean everything. Probably even the *fact* that your daughter is dead."

That made his wrists burn. It couldn't be. That was years ago, decades ago. Doru's grasp—or Alyssa's—whoever the demon was, their reach couldn't stretch that far? Joseph had had a life, a daughter, a marriage—one he'd admittedly wasted away with booze, rage, and self-harm, but still. Could it all be a lie?

"Are you . . ." he stammered. "Are you saying that if we get out of here, Mel could be alive?"

"I'm not promising anything, but maybe, yes." Alyssa nodded, her eyes glistening. "Please take me to him."

"Okay," Joseph whispered. "After we've eaten, okay?"

"Sure."

They ate and drank in silence. Baker and Carver never moved. Like they said, those were their spots, but one after another the rest of the guests shuffled out. Bryan came and took their plates, a weird smile on his face, as always.

"Can I get you anything else, Mr. Podwall?"

Joseph shook his head.

"What about you, Alyssa?"

She said no as well, and Bryan disappeared as fast as he'd come.

"So that's why Bryan never eats, even though you're both staff? Because he's like us?"

"Yes, I think so. I'm not quite sure."

"So, what is this?" Joseph waved at the room around them, at everything. "An illusion? Is any of this even real?" He grazed a wrist with a finger. *Am I real?*

"I . . . Joseph, it's difficult to explain. Can you please take me to Doru? Let me show you instead. Can we go now?"

"Okay, fine. I'll take you to him."

They stood to leave together, went out through the reception, and began ascending the stairs side by side.

"He's not in his room, is he?"

"Not 532, no. He's on my floor. Right next to my room, actually."

"Huh." Alyssa exhaled. "I'd never have found him if I had to go through every single room."

"Actually, you've—" Joseph stopped himself. "There's something you should know. He probably doesn't look like you think."

"What do you mean?"

"How old do you think he is?"

"His mid-twenties, I'd guess, why?"

"Let's just say he's much younger now. You'll see soon enough."

As Joseph arrived on the seventh floor again, a melancholy descended over him. A last hurrah before going home. He was thankful for the sensation, because he was sick and tired of going up and down those stairs. Whatever was going on, he hoped with all his soul that Alyssa could stop it.

They passed Joseph's room with a sense of moving in slow motion. Joseph's head turned, looking at the golden numbers of room 704. For a second, he thought Alyssa's reflection in them was that of another person, another woman. Similar but older. The moment was brief, it didn't even have time to scare Joseph. When he turned to look at her, she was her regular self.

Stopping outside 708, Joseph nodded toward the door.

"Here it is. Doru is hiding in here."

Alyssa raised her hand to knock, but Joseph stopped her. "Just a second. Remember the boy at breakfast? And the young woman, his mother?"

"Yeah, Kyle?"

"No. That's Doru. That's his disguise. As you said, he can do things, change things."

A frown entangled her face. "Are you joking with me?" She didn't wait for an answer, before knocking hard on the door. "Doru! Are you in there?" Knocking again with one hand, she fished out a set of keys from her pocket with the other, scowling hard at Joseph. "You idiot."

"What?"

"The couple at breakfast, that's not Doru. They live on the second floor. I talk to them every day. What the fuck, Joseph?"

Another knock before she turned the lock and wrestled with the door. It flung open. To Joseph's surprise, Alyssa managed to grab it before it smacked against the ceiling.

The room was dark. The bed was untouched, and the lights were off. Joseph carefully swung the door to the bathroom open. It was almost completely closed—maybe Doru hid in there? But it was just as empty and dark.

Alyssa turned on the small desk lamp, and Joseph noticed the lamp on the nightstand wasn't there anymore.

"Well? He's not here, is he?" She crossed her arms. "And don't give me another story about how he's the boy. He's not. But it was a good lie to serve you, makes you think he's been sitting there every day, all the time."

"How can you know that's not the case? Even if you've seen them living on the second floor, couldn't he have done exactly what I said?"

Alyssa sighed, sitting down on the perfectly made bed. "Because the kid and the woman have been here since before Doru, or—I'm not even sure there was a place here before Doru —but since his arrival at least. I shared a table with him while they were next to me. He might have used them as a disguise, but he's not him."

"Where is he then?"

"I don't know," Alyssa shrugged. "Did you alert him we were coming?"

"No, not at all."

"Are you sure? If he was in here, he must also have left from here—did you say anything to him about me?"

"Not that I can think of, but hang on a minute." Joseph took a seat by the desk, the same one as when he was there talking to Doru. "You said you would explain things to me when we came up here, and I'm sorry Doru isn't here, but I need an explanation."

He held his hands out in front of Alyssa, making sure she understood what he was asking, and she nodded.

"First of all, what is this place? Because it's not a hotel. Haunted or not, this is some next-level shit. What's going on?"

"It's not a hotel. Of course, it's not. But at the same time, it is, just look." She waved a hand around the room. "But it's not really. Doru's probably had this dance with you already, but there's no leaving, there's no coming, people just appear."

Joseph could only nod his agreement.

"But Doru will have you believe it's me who's keeping you here, and it's not. I promise. I'm trying to help us all leave. It's Doru who's keeping us all here, because this is his—" She pursed her lips looking around the room.

*She looks so afraid.*

"Manifestation. His illusion. I don't know entirely. I'm stuck here too."

"How did we end up in here?" Joseph asked. "Why am I here? Why is *anyone* here?"

"Because Doru wants us here, in one way or another. Even me. He must have some interest in my help, but he's convinced himself that I'm trying to hurt him. But I'm not, I'm really not."

"How did we end up here?" Joseph asked again. "Are we— is this real? I'm . . . I'm not quite sure what I'm asking. If this is a simulation, or whatever the fuck it is, how are we in it? Am I lying in Doru's house with wires in my head?" Joseph raised his voice, shouting at Alyssa. "How am I here?"

"I don't know," Alyssa said, one single tear crawling down her stern face. "I have no idea."

"Fuck this," Joseph muttered. "You go back to the dining lounge, wait for me there."

He got out of his chair and left before Alyssa could respond. He was about to head down the hallway toward the stairwell, but turned in the opposite direction, further in. Joseph hammered on the first door he saw, 709.

"Doru? Get the fuck out here, stop hiding!" he yelled. He was going to force him out.

"Alyssa is gone, I'm sorry I brought her up."

He pounded on 710, 711, and 712. "Where the fuck did you go?"

Striding down the hallway, he felt like he grew larger and larger, propped up by the rage inside him. That, or the hallway was shrinking around him. He was a lumbering giant, waddling through the halls, pounding on doors, screaming for Doru to come out. Joseph soon found himself at the end of the hallway—or rather—the start of it. The stairwell loomed in front of him.

"Doru?" he screamed as he carried on down the stairs. "Where the fuck are you, you rat-bastard? You're keeping everyone hostage here, come out and face us, you child!"

Joseph kept at it through all the floors, spiraling through hallway after hallway, stairwell after stairwell. The rage was building up inside him. He wished he had one of his razor blades with him. His hands kept searching his pockets, even though he knew all the blades were in his room.

At the last door on the second floor, he heard crying. Not very strange considering he'd been running through every single floor, hammering on the doors and shouting. The crying brought him back to reality—this must be where the real woman and child lived.

The woman sniffled as she opened the door carefully. "Yes?"

"Is . . . Is Doru here?" Joseph asked.

"No, it's just me and my son, Kyle."

Little Kyle came walking up behind his momma, grabbing her around the knee, shielding himself.

"Hey little guy." Joseph bent down, smiling, trying to steady his breath. "I'm looking for my friend, Doru. Have you seen him?"

"What's he look like?"

"Uhm, about as old as you, maybe? As tall as you."

"No, haven't seen him—I'm the only boy here. And there's one girl."

Joseph swallowed. *Mel probably.*

He didn't have time for more of this. "What about a grown man. Tall like me, but younger. Much younger."

"Maybe." Kyle giggled. "There was a man outside. He went up the stairs."

"Outside? In the yard?"

"Yeah."

*The stone steps in the courtyard.*

"Okay, that's enough," Kyle's mother said. "Please leave us alone."

"Thank you, ma'am, I'm sorry to—" but she shut the door in his face.

Whatever was behind the door on top of the small staircase in the courtyard, it was the only place in this whole goddamn world he hadn't been. Maybe that's where Doru had gone. And maybe that was the clue to ending this.

Continuing his stampede downstairs, he cast Bryan a hard glance just as the young man looked up at him, which apparently was enough to shut him up.

Joseph went by the dining room to see Alyssa sitting where he'd asked her to wait. She seemed anxious as he strode over.

"I haven't found him yet, but I'm going to."

"Great, come get me when—"

"What are you going to do to him? Really? I need to be able to tell him, and no I won't be getting you. I'll bring him here."

"I'm really just going to talk to him. We need to sit down and chat. I'll make him see what's real and what's not."

"Do you promise?"

"Yes."

Joseph turned and strode off, catching Baker and Carver's creepy smiles in the bar mirror as he turned.

*What are they up to? Why do they look so suspicious?*

Walking through the large hallway that led to the courtyard, he noticed a bench in the white, sterile hallway. The one he'd sat on, waiting, before he identified Mel's body all those years ago. In the ballroom he saw the shadows of people sitting at the round tables. They were barely visible, like lingering smoke, but they were clearly the outlines of people. At first it scared him. Until he recognized them. Himself, his ex-wife, friends of the family. Joseph stopped, taking it in, trying to remember that day, but it felt so distant.

He turned the corner, carrying on toward the heavy doors. They opened on their own this time, before Joseph even touched them. It didn't surprise him. He was invited to come after all, the last stop before the end. No winds blew through the courtyard that served as Mel's final resting place. The sun dripped down upon him, hovering over her delicate gravestone.

"Hey, sweetie," he whispered, caressing the top of the gravestone before walking across the meadow to where the small staircase curled around the circular wall of the hotel.

He took the stone steps slowly, one at a time. They stood like horizontal pillars, jutting out of the face of the wall, leading up to that small inconspicuous door on the middle of the wall.

At the top, he stopped to admire the view, and to his surprise it was back to being a courtyard. No beautiful meadow with a lonely grave—just an overgrown courtyard, with a broken fountain.

Joseph turned toward the door, unsure whether to barge in or knock first. It was a single, brown, wooden door, unremarkable in its appearance. No intricate carving, no golden adornment. A simple door.

*No illusions this time?*

He grabbed the door handle, clenching his fist around it. The room he entered was long and narrow. Dark, with sunlight beaming in from somewhere above. He couldn't see the end, nor the sides. The floor was rough concrete, no ugly carpet, no creaking wood. Joseph's steps echoed off the walls as he walked in.

As his eyes adjusted, he saw them. Right there on the floor in front of him, Doru—the real Doru, in his mid-twenties, sitting on the floor. He sat cross-legged, wearing nothing but tan pants and a white t-shirt. His dark, wavy hair shielded his eyes.

Next to him was Mel. Real-life, five-year-old Mel. They were drawing with crayons, as they had been in the dining room. Joseph realized it wasn't *he* who had been sitting with his daughter. It wasn't his younger self he'd seen in the bar mirror when his body had changed. It was Doru.

"Hey, Joseph. Sorry I ran earlier. I wasn't ready to face Alyssa yet." Doru's voice was calm and somber as he picked up a crayon and drew a few lines on Mel's piece of paper. Joseph hardly heard him, his focus was all on Mel.

"Baby girl," he said, tears overflowing in his eyes, squatting down next to them. "How are you doing?"

She looked up at him, giggled, but didn't say anything and went back to her crayons.

"Why are you doing this, Doru? Why are you making me see her?"

"I don't think I am," he said, drawing a few red circles on Mel's paper. "I thought it was you?"

"If it was me, she wouldn't be five years old. If it was me, I'd see her again one last time before I lost her. Holding her, hugging her, telling her how much I love her.

Streams were running down Joseph's cheeks, and for the

first time since he could remember, he didn't long for the razor blade. Sadness washed over him. It felt cleansing.

"I'm sorry, Joseph," Doru said, looking away. "I'm sorry about Mel, about everything."

"Don't be. Just get us out of here. Alyssa says she can help. She says you're keeping us all here, and that she can make it stop. But you have to talk to her."

"I'm sorry about Mel," Doru said again, ignoring what Joseph had said. "I never meant to deceive you."

"It's okay, Doru. Come with me. Snap your fingers and . . ." He didn't want to say it, didn't want it to go away just yet. "Just come, let's go."

"She was never nineteen," Doru whispered, finally meeting Joseph's gaze.

Joseph's stomach dropped. "What?"

"I—I'm not sure why she's here. But she was never nineteen, Joseph."

"Yes, she was! She was an adult, in college, about to move out, she—" but as he said it, he knew it wasn't true.

Doru shook his head, stroking Mel's blonde hair gently. "No, Joseph. She wasn't."

"Yes, she was!" Joseph's voice echoed through the dark room.

"She was only five. She only ever got to five." Tears streamed down Doru's face. "And she wasn't your daughter. She was mine."

Mel disappeared, in a puff of smoke.

Joseph stumbled backward, grabbing the sides of his head. "What did you do?"

The dark gray smoke hovered for a bit before dispersing between them, leaving only Joseph and Doru staring at each other. Even the crayons were gone. Joseph shook, unable to find words to accompany his heaving breath.

"After you came to see me yesterday, when we talked about her, you reminded me," Doru began. "I'm not sure why I hid her as yours, but I'm sorry. I'm sorry for deceiving you, sorry for making you feel all that pain."

"But how could . . ." Joseph didn't understand. He'd been carrying that photograph for years, from when they were in Paris. He had recognized her gravestone just like it was, in the meadow where she lay. "No, you're—"

Doru reached up to Joseph's breast pocket, fishing the photograph out as if by magic. "I'm not sure what you thought this looked like, but look at it now."

There was no Louvre in the background. It was someone's backyard. There was a tree and a poorly constructed tree house. It wasn't nineteen-year-old Melanie standing on the right the way Joseph had remembered. It was the little girl, the five-year-old who'd been sitting in front of him only a minute ago. And next to her, on the left, a young Doru.

"Mel was my little treasure," Doru sighed, turning the photograph toward himself.

As Joseph heard the words leave Doru's mouth, the air knocked out of him. His lungs burned as he tried to gasp for breath. His chest threatened to collapse in on itself. He wanted to get angry, to shout and scream and hit things, but he couldn't find the energy for it. There was rage and anger every-where inside of him, but no power behind it.

None of this was his pain to bear.

It wasn't his life.

Not anymore. Not ever, apparently.

Finally, he managed to breathe. A raw and ice-cold breath hurt on the way down, but soothed as it settled. There was a sadness within him, a heavy grief, but without the idea of Melanie being his daughter, there was nothing for it to latch onto.

There was a gut-punch of emotion running through him, but no gut. His wrists didn't burn anymore.

*I never came here for that.*

"When I lost her, I lost everything. Everything crumbled to pieces."

"I'm sorry, Doru," Joseph whispered. "I'm sorry. But let me take you to Alyssa. Let's sit down and talk, get us all out of this hell."

"All right, Joseph," Doru said, looking down into the ground. "Sure, let's go."

They got up and walked down the dark room, toward the small door.

"Is this where you've been hiding?" Joseph asked, looking around at the darkness as they approached the door. Doru's head shifted from side to side.

"In a way I think this is the only place I haven't been hiding. I'm not sure that makes any sense."

After opening the door for Doru, Joseph was surprised to be standing at the bottom of the stairwell. He turned around, assuming he'd see the lobby behind them, complete with Bryan's stupid grin, but it was just an empty room.

"What the hell?"

"Don't worry about it, Joe," Doru said, starting up the steps. "We have to make the climb. Sorry, the elevator is out of order."

As soon as Doru said it, Joseph heard the whirring and clanking of machinery, yet he couldn't see the elevator anywhere.

They went up and up the stairs. Joseph wanted so badly to turn, go back downstairs to emerge in the lobby. That's where he knew Alyssa was, but Doru assured him this was the right way.

"When you've been in here as long as I have, when you've

started to understand the ebb and flow of things around here, you get used to the shifts and changes. The hotel isn't evil, you know. There's nothing inherently malevolent in its creation or existence. It takes some getting used to. You've heard the siren calls, haven't you?"

Joseph thought back to the times he had seen the old maid and when Alyssa had morphed into Glenn, screeching at the top of her lungs. "Yeah," he nodded.

"That freaked me out the first few times. More than the first time, honestly. But like I said, you get used to it. You get used to the breathing of this place, its pulse. Once you do that, you can start to control it."

"Like you do?"

Doru smiled. "Yeah, like I do."

"What about Baker and Carver? They seem to have been here a while. How come they can't affect it like you?"

Doru squinted at the ceiling lights of the sixth floor as they rounded the corner. "I'm not sure. I think maybe they gave up. Or gave in. I'm not sure. I feel like they're in the same boat as me, but without the wind in their back. They don't have the same will or the same power. Who knows?"

They ascended the last flight of stairs, stepped up onto the seventh floor. The whole building shifted as they stepped down into the hotel lobby. Joseph's stomach revolted and he buckled over, grabbing himself by his knees. "What the fuck?"

Doru stepped in front of him. "Yeah, I'm sorry, it does that sometimes."

Doru held out his hand, but Joseph waved it away. As he struggled to stand, he saw Bryan smile at him from the reception. He didn't say anything, just nodded. Doru hesitated in front of the archway to the dining lounge which gave Joseph time to catch up.

"You ready?" Joseph asked, to which Doru exhaled and gave a single, deep nod.

As they entered the dining lounge, Alyssa rose from her seat to meet them.

"Doru, finally. It's good to see you again, thanks for coming." She smiled wide. "Please have a seat."

It wasn't the same old, rectangular dining table they were sitting down at. It was a desk, like an office desk. Alyssa on one side, him and Doru on the other.

"How are you feeling, Doru?" Alyssa asked.

"Nervous."

"Why?"

"Because I'm afraid you'll take everything away from me."

"Like what?"

"This place. Mel. My friends, Baker, Carver, and Joseph. Everything."

"And you don't want that to happen?"

"Of course not." Doru shifted in his seat. "I'm happy here. Spending time with the others, sitting at the bar, playing with my girl."

"But you know we can't stay."

Joseph kept turning his head between the two of them.

"Why not?" Doru asked.

"Because it's not fair. Not to me, not to Joseph." She gestured an open palm. "Not to Baker and Carver."

Joseph hadn't noticed until now, but they were still there, at the end of the room. In the reflection of the bar mirror, Joseph saw the two men raise their coffee cups.

"Keep us out of this, bitch," Baker yelled cheerfully before he took a sip.

Joseph was a bit taken aback by his outburst, but Alyssa didn't seem fazed at all. Her focus was on Doru.

"Is it fair to go back? Why is that better? Back to where Mel is dead, to where—" Doru choked.

Joseph felt his own throat tightening. Doru wasn't the powerful mastermind behind the hotel's illusions anymore. He was just a scared young man.

"It might not be what you want, but yes, it is fair," Alyssa said. "To go back there, where we're not lying to ourselves. To where we can learn to cope with what is."

Doru craned his neck toward Joseph, almost unnaturally so. Joseph instinctively jerked back. Alyssa also turned her head toward him.

"Do you think it's fair that we have to go back, Joe?" Doru asked in a monotonous voice.

"I don't know, depends on where we're going, I suppose? But I know damn well I don't want to stay in this house of smoke and mirrors where stairs lead both up and down at the same time, where floors change, where rooms are all the same but different. It's exhausting, it's chaotic, it's—"

"What if I told you . . ." Doru wiped a hand across his tear-stained cheek. "What if I told you that, going back—the place Alyssa wants us all to go—is where we just were."

*What?* "What do you mean? The stairwell?"

"That black, empty room. Where you never see the walls at either end. Just a small beam of light, a door, and a cold floor. Nothing but the memory of my dead daughter to keep me company." Doru was tearing up again. "And the pain. The unending pain, all the time. And the darkness. So much darkness. Would you go back to that, Joseph? If that was the reality waiting for you, would you return to that? Or would you spend the rest of your life here?"

Joseph couldn't wrap his head around it. Why would that be the only option? *How* was that the only option? His wrists throbbed again for a moment, but knowing that Mel wasn't real—at least not to him—knowing that it wasn't *his* daughter who died, had changed him. All he wanted to do was leave.

"I don't know, Doru, but I agree with Alyssa. It's not fair to keep us here."

"Fine," Doru looked back at Alyssa again, sneering. "But I don't think it's fair that I have to go back."

Alyssa gasped and reached out to grab him. "Doru, don't!" she yelled, but it was too late. He was gone. Just like that, he was left sitting alone with Alyssa, staring at the empty seat.

"Well . . . Did that go according to plan?" Joseph asked.

Alyssa sighed. Her hands were still outstretched toward where Doru had been sitting. "What do you think?"

"I think no, it didn't, because you're trying to force him to do something he doesn't want to."

"What do you suggest?" Alyssa raised her voice slightly.

"I think that whatever it is you're trying to get him to do, you're trying too hard. If you want someone to do something, don't push them in one direction. You're just going to make them run twice as fast in the other."

"Well excuse me, Mr. Therapist," she huffed.

"You need to convince him that *he* wants to do this. Make him think it's his idea."

"And how, pray tell, are we going to go about that?"

"I don't fucking know." Joseph shrugged, leaning back in his chair. "This is your gig, not mine. I'm just in it for the ride."

"Are you sure?" Alyssa asked with a frown.

"What do you mean, *am I sure*?"

"You don't think you have a bigger role in this?"

"What role would that be?"

"You're the only one who's been able to get through to Doru. To find him, to convince him to at least come here. Why do you think that is?"

"No idea," Joseph said, shrugging again.

"Well, get an idea. We need to talk to him again. We need to find him again. That's your job in this. Now go, scram."

She waved him away, and for some reason, Joseph felt compelled to get up and leave. He started walking upstairs. The same unbearable trod up the hundreds of steps. The elevator hummed its mechanical tune alongside him as he rounded every landing on each floor. Joseph didn't care enough to get angry. Walking down the hall on the seventh floor, he stopped, closed his eyes, willing room 704 to be there. Turning sideways, he opened his eyes, and it was right there.

*Neat trick, Doru.*

The shards of paperclips on the floor of his room immediately drew his eye. Joseph bent down to pick them up.

"I'd forgotten about you guys," he mused, studying them in the palm of his hands before putting them in his pocket.

The photograph wasn't on the nightstand, and he instinctively clasped a hand to his heart. It wasn't in his shirt pocket either, he remembered, because it wasn't his to carry.

It was Doru's.

He laid down on the bed for a while, hands intertwined behind his head. This existence wasn't so bad—who wouldn't love to stay in a hotel all the time?

With the burden of his daughter's death lifted, he didn't feel like looking for the razor blade, didn't feel like ending it all. Maybe Alyssa was mistaken, maybe they could have an all right time here.

"You know that's not true," Doru said, appearing in the chair by the desk.

"Jesus fucking Christ!" Joseph grabbed at his galloping heart. "What the hell, Doru? Don't you ever do that again." Joseph sat up, rubbing his face.

"I like your jacket," Doru said, smiling, looking down at the leather jacket where it hung on the back of Doru's chair.

"Thanks, I guess. It belonged to my dad," he began, but as

he heard the words, they sounded wrong to him. "It belonged to your dad, didn't it?"

Doru's smile grew wider. "Maybe. I'm not sure anymore."

"This as well?" Joseph asked, holding up his wrist, making the German watch dangle.

"Definitely looks familiar . . ."

It dawned on Joseph that that was another burden that wasn't his to carry. "I'm—I'm sorry about your father. About everything he did."

"Don't apologize, Joseph. It's not yours to worry about."

Joseph forced a painful smile, bobbing his head. "Why'd you disappear like that? Alyssa wanted to talk to you."

"She wants me out of here. Forgotten and buried."

"Are you sure about that?"

"Remind me, when I told you what going back was like, did she argue? No, she didn't. Because that's what it is, for all of us. That cold, empty room."

"So, it's either that, or this? A fucked up hotel, forever?"

"Pretty much."

Joseph sighed. "Why am I here, Doru?" he asked eventually. "If I understand correctly, you're here to escape something, but why am *I* here? What's dragged me into this? I don't know anything about going back. I don't know anything about anything. Frank brought me here, and that's all I remember."

"You were my friend," Doru said, smiling. He looked over Joseph's head as if deep in thought. "I think I brought you here, not Frank. Just like I brought Baker and Carver. I think I brought everyone here."

"It's true what Alyssa is saying then. It's not fair to us, that you've put us here."

Doru's gaze hit the floor. "Maybe not."

"What's it going to take to convince you to let us go?"

"I don't know. I . . . Even if I could, I'm not sure how to release you."

Joseph sat up, stretching his back. "What do you mean?"

"Well, you found me in there. In the empty space. Yet, here you all are, regardless. Even if I go back, I don't know how to end all this." Doru gestured at the walls. "I don't know how to break it down."

"Have you tried?" Joseph suggested. "Have you tried . . . I don't know, giving it up?"

"No, I'm too afraid. I locked myself in here, to see Mel, to be with her. I miss her so much. Why did she have to leave?"

"I assume," Joseph hesitated, looking for the right words. "I assume the story I know about her is the one that you know. She died?"

Doru sniffled. "She was killed."

Just like Joseph remembered—or thought he remembered. It still stung even though he had no relation to Mel. The thought of losing someone he cared about sparked a sharp pain in his chest.

"Maybe she's what's keeping you here? Maybe you're hiding away in here, whatever this place is, because you're not ready to face the loss?"

Doru looked at him, almost suspiciously, as if he saw through to what Joseph's real intentions were. "Maybe. But even if I am, how do I know this isn't the better alternative?"

"You don't," Joseph said quickly. "You fucking don't. And three hours ago, when I thought Mel was my daughter that I'd lost, I wasn't fucking happy about dealing with it either. I know what you're feeling, literally, because you made me feel it." Saying it out loud made Joseph wonder. "How did you feel, back then? When she was mine, I mean?"

"Not a thing," Doru confessed. "Probably like you do now, I'm guessing. Very little at least."

"So, how about you give her back to me again. You've done it before, you can do it again, can't you? Make Mel my daughter and let me take the burden off you. Then we can go back down to Alyssa and deal with this. Maybe you'll think differently about it without your grief hanging over you."

"Even if I could give her back to you, which I don't think I'm able to, I'm not sure what would happen to you if I did. I don't think you'd understand what was going on, I don't think you'd be able to remember what the real truth was. You'd probably try and kill yourself again," Doru said, nodding toward the suitcase.

"You knew about that?" Joseph said, his voice rising. That meant that his pain, his suffering, was all Doru's fault.

"Yeah, I did. I'm sorry. I didn't know that's how you would react, that that's how you'd try to deal with it. That's why I kept bringing you back."

Joseph rose from the bed in harmony with his rising voice, screaming at Doru. "You're responsible for bringing me back to life? When I woke up downstairs, sitting at the table?"

"Yeah." Doru shuddered. "I'm—"

"How many times?" Joseph yelled. "How many times have I killed myself for nothing?"

Doru cowered. "Just two, I think. I'm sorry, Joseph."

Joseph hoisted him up by the neck of his shirt. "You've killed me twice?" He couldn't believe what he was hearing. Since he'd arrived at this God-forsaken place all he could think about was dying, and now he realized it was because Doru couldn't deal with his own guilt. "You're a dick, Doru. You know that? A dick and a coward."

"I know," he sobbed. "I just don't want to go back. It hurts too damn much."

"What about Baker and Carver. Have you used their lives as well, to your liking? Forced them to kill themselves? Fucked them over?" Joseph let Doru fall back into the chair before leaning down to get in his face. "Huh?"

"No, they're here for company, I haven't—"

"Let's go down and talk to them, we haven't heard what they have to say yet."

"I'm not going. If Alyssa is there she'll try and—"

"Listen here, you little shit. I'm sick of this bullshit. I'm going to go downstairs to check if Alyssa is there, and as soon as she's not, you're going to do your little magic trick and appear downstairs. Capiche?"

Joseph headed for the door without giving him a chance to reply. Just as he was about to exit to the hallway, he looked at the bathroom door, slightly ajar. He could see the white, dirty tiles on the floor inside. Grabbing the door handle, he slammed the door, closed his eyes, opened it and stepped through.

"Good afternoon, sir," Bryan greeted him as Joseph stepped through the front doors of the hotel.

*I could get used to the magic though, it's pretty handy.*

Joseph ignored Bryan completely. Striding through the dining room he saw Alyssa's hopeful gaze.

"Fuck off, Alyssa," he said casually. "Doru is coming, best you're not here then." He sensed she wanted to interject but she stood up to leave after a thoughtful second.

"Make room, boys," Joseph said walking up to the bars. "I found your pal, and as you know, we have a lot to talk about."

Carver moved to the right, making room for Joseph to take the middle seat, like before. He was about to ask Carver to jump another seat over, making room for Doru between them, when the man in question walked in behind the bar.

"What can I get you fellows?" Doru asked, wearing a fancy white shirt, doled up to be a bartender.

"Answers," Joseph said, before Baker and Carver each ordered a beer.

"About time we got something other than coffee in this joint," Baker said.

Joseph wanted to tell them there wasn't time for drinks, but instead figured he'd have one as well. He wasn't even sure if he was an alcoholic anymore, considering so much of what he thought was his life had been a figment of Doru's imagination.

"So," Joseph said after a hefty sip of his frothy drink. It tasted like heaven. "Doru's keeping us all here against our will, and he's refusing to let us leave." He put his glass down with a clank on the bar.

"We're stuck here no matter what," Baker said, taking a couple of sips of his drink, fishing out a smoke from his pocket. "If we're here or there, it doesn't really matter to us, does it?" He looked at Carver in the mirror.

"No, sir. Doesn't matter to me. I'm happy."

Joseph looked between the two of them. "How can you be? He's robbing you of your life, of your experiences, keeping you here in this . . . whatever the hell this is!"

"Are you so sure about that, Joe?" Baker asked. "How can you be certain the alternative is better? If you were going to hell, wouldn't you rather stay in limbo?"

Joseph wasn't sure how to respond. "I don't know what the alternative is, but the fact that we're kept here against our will should be argument enough!" Joseph couldn't believe what he was hearing. "Don't you want to be free?"

"Maybe," Carver mused. "But at what price? Would you rather be free and cold, or caged and warm?"

Joseph thought about it. "Free and cold. I'd rather step outside and drop dead instantly instead of being cooped up in here, not having any choice in the matter." He looked hard at Doru.

"Joseph, listen." Doru poured another drink for Carver who

had somehow finished his. "We all have our things to deal with. Alyssa's trying to help, but who says she's going to be able to? I can make everyone very comfortable here." He gestured at the bar with a cheeky smile. "We can have a pretty good time, don't you think?"

"But you're not having a good time, are you, Doru? You're using this as a façade, as a shield around your own reality. Sure, Bert and Ernie here are happy with a constant flow of cigarettes and booze, because they have no choice. They're pawns." Joseph pointed a thick finger at Doru. "But you have a choice. You're choosing to let this happen, and you can choose to let go of it."

"Why are you taking her side?" Doru asked.

"Why wouldn't I? Alyssa isn't the beast you think she is. Sounds like she's trying to do what's best for you, while at the same time getting us all out of here!" Joseph leaned over the bar as he shouted.

"I think you'd be happy here, if you gave it a chance," Doru said, looking at Baker and Carver for affirmation, who both gave a silent tip of the head while enjoying their drinks.

"I could say the exact same thing about you leaving, about you giving up this whole charade."

"But I don't want to."

"And I don't want to stay!"

"Even if I did, how would I leave?" Doru asked. "Like I said, I've tried going back. This place doesn't necessarily cease to exist. This reality is still there when I go back to that cold, empty room."

"That's why we need to talk to Alyssa, to figure this out. Going in there clearly isn't enough, maybe you need to confront something, maybe you need to confront Mel—"

Doru's expression grew hard. "No. I came here to get away from it all. I can't bear losing her again."

"You don't have to. You just have to accept that you already lost—"

"No, I won't." Doru shook his head. "I'm not going to do it."

Joseph stood from his stool in anger. "Well, maybe it's not up to you."

"You underestimate me, Joseph. Everything in here is up to me."

With that, Joseph was suddenly back in his room, lying on his bed.

"Coward," Joseph grumbled as he got out of bed and headed downstairs.

Doru wasn't there when he came back, and Baker and Carver shook their heads when Joseph met their eyes in the mirror.

"How did it go without me?" Alyssa asked from the corner, bringing Joseph's attention to her. He walked over and took a seat.

"Not better. He's very insistent on staying."

"I'm well aware," she said.

"Is it true what he said? About going back. Is the alternative that empty room out by the courtyard?"

"I'm not sure. I think so. For him at least. But I also think it is what he wants it to be. Kind of like here, but without dragging us down with him."

"What does that mean?"

"That yes, if he goes back, that's what he goes to, but it doesn't have to be that horrible. Baker and Carver have been making it work for years."

"And they're in the same situation? You're sure of that?" Joseph asked.

"I think so, but you should ask them. I don't think Doru's problem is about where he's going to end up, it's more about *why* he's going to be there."

"What's that supposed to mean?" Joseph groaned. "Why does everyone in this goddamn illusion talk in fucking riddles?"

"Because none of us know what's going on. Only Doru does, and I don't think even he wants to admit it to himself."

"But Doru said he's tried going back, and it doesn't work. This illusion doesn't disappear. How do we fix that?"

"I don't think Doru has really tried going back." Alyssa hesitated a bit, looking at Carver and Baker in the corner of her eyes. "I don't think he's ever given up on this side of the story, do you know what I mean?"

Joseph sighed. "No, I have absolutely no fucking clue what you mean, but by all means, carry on."

"Even when Doru goes back to that room, he doesn't give up on everything else. He clings to it, like a safety net. Keeping it on standby so he can disappear into himself again. Hide away again."

"So, we need to make him let go? Properly, I mean. Give up on all of this?"

"Yeah."

"Okay," Joseph said, pounding a fist on the table between them. "Step one, figure out why Doru is afraid of going back, and step two, convince him to let go."

"There you have it," Alyssa said.

"What about everyone else? You, me, Glenn, the boys?" Joseph pointed to Baker and Carver in the bar. "What happens to us when I make Doru let go?" He wasn't sure he wanted to hear the answer. What if even then he couldn't leave?

"Nothing, Joseph. Nothing happens to us. Make Doru let go, and you'll end this."

"Are you certain?"

Alyssa sighed. "I am. It's all Doru. When he goes back,

everything goes back. No pain, no suffering, no illusions. All of it will fade. I promise."

"Fine. I'll handle it then. Make me a drink first? One of those whiskey things you made me earlier?"

"Sure, join me at the bar."

Joseph followed Alyssa over. She went behind the bar and found the bottle she'd used the first day, a shaker, and some lime. Joseph didn't sit with Baker and Carver this time, instead deciding to have his drink in peace before he began the final chapter of his stay at The Gate.

He knew how to end it now. He finally figured it out. All he had to do was finish his drink, ask Baker and Carver about why Doru was so scared to go back—he thought he already knew what they would say—then he'd go find Doru and be done with it.

"Will I see you again after this?"

"I don't think so, Joseph," Alyssa said, shaking his drink. She found a tall glass for him under the bar, setting it down on a small white napkin, a few ice cubes in the bottom. "I think that if you do whatever it is you think you're capable of doing, that will be it. Sorry."

"I'm sorry too. I'd love to have spent more time with you, but maybe not here."

Alyssa laughed. "Yeah, maybe not here. This place has a strange effect on people."

"You can say that again." Joseph thought about all the lost time, the changing architecture, his appearance. "And it's all Doru?"

"It's all Doru. This is his place, in a sense. All of it, his own."

"Must be nice," Joseph mused, grabbing hold of the glass as Alyssa poured, "to have your own little sanctuary."

"Yeah, complete with a bunch of unwilling prisoners."

"As opposed to willing prisoners?" Joseph chuckled.

"Yeah, as opposed to that. How's the drink?"

"About as shit as the first time you made it." He put the glass down in front of him, half-empty. "You still don't know what it is, do you?"

"Hell, I'm not even sure if it exists. You could be drinking battery acid for all I know."

"Pretty tasty for battery acid." Joseph winked, chugging down the last of the drink.

"Are you sure you know what to do?" Alyssa splayed her hands out on the bar, leaning in toward him.

"Yeah, I think I finally understand it. I think I finally understand this place. Why I came here, why Doru needed me here."

"And that is?"

"That, my good woman, is too complicated to explain. But I'll let you know if I'm wrong."

"How will you know? If you're wrong, I mean," she asked.

Joseph shrugged. "If I'm wrong, I'll meet you for lunch tomorrow, again."

"Sounds good. I'll be waiting. And if you don't fail?"

"If I don't fail, we won't be needing lunch tomorrow, Alyssa. Don't worry. I've got a plan."

He stood up, giving her one last nod, a goodbye without really saying farewell. He understood now—both where he was, and why, and what it all meant.

"Boys," Joseph said, walking slowly over to Baker and Carver, still drinking the beers Doru had poured them earlier. The glasses looked like they would never be empty. "Baker, Carver, it's been a pleasure."

"You're going to go take care of it then?" Baker asked with a wicked grin.

"I think I am," Joseph said, looking back at Alyssa, who looked sad where she stood at the end of the bar. "Alyssa gave me a few pointers. There's just one thing I need to know, and I think you two are the ones who can help me."

"And what's that?" Carver asked, taking a hearty sip of his brew.

"Doru isn't scared of going back, because like you both know, going back isn't so bad. You get used to it, don't you?"

Baker cocked his head and pursed his lips, clearly not opposed to the statement.

"Doru is scared to go back because of the reasons that put him there. One of you care to tell me what those are?"

"Listen, Joe. I don't know why Doru ended up where he did. He never told us, he never told any of us anything."

"There must be someone who knows. What about Bryan?" Joseph suggested.

"Someone does," Carver agreed. "But it's not Bryan."

"Who then?"

"I think you know," Baker said, turning back toward the bar to carry on staring into the mirror.

Other than Doru, there was only one other person who knew why they were all there. *He did.*

"Bryan!" Joseph called, leaving the dining room. Bryan stood at the ready when Joseph entered the reception. "I need to see him," Joseph said, pointing at the back office.

"See who?" Bryan asked, a tremble in his voice.

"Cut the shit, Bryan. I know he's in there. He's been there all the time, I know it. You—or Doru—hid him from me last time I was in there. I need to see Frank, and I need to see him *now.*"

"Frank's not back there, Frank's the driver—"

"Bryan, step out of the way," Joseph said, beginning to walk around the reception desk.

Joseph took a step into the doorway of the back office, looking into the same depressing room he'd seen earlier, the one where Bryan appeared to eat, sleep, and live. Joseph could tell Bryan wanted to stop him as he grabbed the door, but the boy stopped himself. Joseph slowly closed the door and knocked on it.

"Don't worry about it, Bry," Joseph said calmly, daring a glance at the boy who took a gentle step backward.

"Yes?" a voice from inside the room called. Joseph opened the door again, and it wasn't the same run-down, messy back-office of the reception.

It was pristine. A dark wooden floor, beautiful green wall-paper—almost new. On the walls were paintings, expensive ones by the look of them. A large mahogany desk stood in the middle of the room, the sides of it lined with filing cabinets. Behind the desk sat a large pudgy man, with slick grey hair on top of his head and a cleanly shaven chin. He reminded Joseph of a better-dressed version of Baker.

"May I come in, sir?" Joseph asked.

"Joseph," the man rumbled. "Sure, come have a seat."

On top of the desk was a golden nameplate that read: *Frank M. Arden.*

"I had a few questions about Doru Amani," Joseph said, easing into the only chair in front of the desk.

"Who?" Frank grunted, nose deep in a newspaper.

"The young guy in room 532. Been the talk of the town around here recently."

"Oh yes, yes," Frank said, hoisting himself out of his chair with a groan, his large gut sagging over the desk. He huffed and puffed as he waddled over to the filing cabinet, pulling out drawer after drawer. "I swear I have his file somewhere. How are you liking it here so far, Joseph?" Frank asked over his shoulder. "Settling in all right?"

Joseph smiled at the corner of his mouth, a stillness washing over him. He finally understood his role in everything

—he understood everyone's role in it. "Yeah, I've been finding my footing."

"Yeah?" Frank turned around with a thin folder in his hands. "That's good. Good they finally sent someone in here to sort out this mess. I can only do so much you know." He laughed, plopping down in his chair as he slapped the folder down in front of Joseph. "It's good to have people like you out there in the field. People who handle the day-to-day, you know?"

"I get it," Joseph said, reaching for the file. He casually put one leg over the other, opening the folder. "This is everything on Doru?"

"Yeah, it's all in there. Take your time with it, but I want it back when you're done."

Joseph read it, and read it again. Doru's life laid bare in front of him. Everything fell into place, just like he knew it would. Doru was hiding, no doubt about it, but Joseph now knew how to get him back.

"What do you think, Frank? You ready to call it a night?" Joseph said, putting the folder back on the desk as he stood up.

"Look at me," Frank said, gesturing to his massive body. "I'm exhausted before lunch, I'm sick and tired of this mess. If you think you know what you're doing, Joseph, by all means, do it."

"All right, Frank. Have a good one," Joseph said as he turned to leave.

"You too," Frank said. "I'm counting on you, Joseph."

"Thanks, Bryan," Joseph said as he stepped out behind the reception. Bryan looked nervous, jittery with anticipation. "Don't be scared, kid. You'll be all right."

"Are you sure?" He was stammering again. "H-how do you know what's going to happen?"

"It's going to be fine, Bry."

Joseph stopped in the middle of the lobby. Through the archway he saw Baker and Carver sitting at the bar, chatting away. Alyssa stood behind it, serving them. Glenn was sitting alone in the corner, like he used to. Clyde and Marcia gave Joseph a small wave from where they sat together, and Kyle and his mom came walking down the stairs, going past Joseph where he stood. Kyle was all smiles and giggles.

*Where do I look for you first?*

He instinctively walked toward the door next to the elevator, to the large hallway leading out to the courtyard. He passed through it all without giving any of it a second glance. The grave wasn't there anymore, just the fountain. Walking up the stone steps he opened the door to the cold, dark room.

Doru sat there on the floor, scribbling on the stone with a piece of chalk.

"What do you want?" Doru asked.

"You know what I want," Joseph said, crossing his arms over his chest. "It's time."

"What?" Doru looked confused, but Joseph knew it wasn't sincere. Joseph grabbed him by the neck of his shirt and pulled him to his feet. "Wait, what are you doing?"

"You know what I'm doing," Joseph answered solemnly, dragging Doru with him toward the door.

"No, let me go!" Doru resisted—punched, kicked, pulled— but nothing would release him from Joseph's grasp.

"It's time to go, Doru, you know that."

"No!" Doru yelled, his face morphing to that of Baker, Carver, and Glenn. Joseph pushed the doors open to the courtyard, dragging Doru down the cold stone steps. "Let me go," Doru wailed. As he screamed, the winds started battering them; the storm that had ravaged the courtyard earlier had returned.

Joseph didn't mind, he hardly even noticed. He dragged

Doru toward the double doors he knew would lead them straight into the lobby, but Doru waved a hand—performing one of his illusions—and the door disappeared. Joseph calmly turned around, heading across the courtyard to the other set of doors.

The winds whipped around them, slapping Joseph across the face, chilling him to the bone. Doru screamed and kicked trying to break free, but Joseph's hold on him was determined. As they passed the fountain, it morphed, became a grave, became a boulder, became Mel. It convulsed into different appearances, never settling on a single image.

"You can stop it now, Doru, it's not going to work."

"No! No, please. Let's talk about it, Joseph please. Don't do this to me!"

"I'm not," Joseph said, opening the double doors, walking slowly through the dreary ballroom. The shadowy figures at the table were people he recognized now. Bryan, Alyssa, Doru, himself. They all changed, wobbled in and out of their forms, becoming Glenn, Baker, Frank. The old maid was there too. The siren howled somewhere in the distance.

"Joseph, please," Doru cried. "I don't want to go."

"Yes, you do," Joseph said, walking down the lonely hallway. The colors on the walls blinked, like traffic lights, ever-changing. Walking through the door at the end, emerging in the lobby, Joseph shifted his grip on Doru's collar slightly, but no matter how much Doru resisted, he couldn't wrestle free of Joseph's hold. Joseph couldn't understand it, he was barely holding on, and Doru was fighting for his life.

"I think we'll head upstairs," Joseph suggested, beginning the long climb up the stairs.

"Please, Joseph. Please stop and think about it! Let me go. We can live like kings in here. I'll share, I'll give you whatever you want."

"Don't bother, Doru. There's no point. You've already chosen."

They rounded the landing on the second floor. Doru continued to struggle in Joseph's grasp, but Joseph was stronger.

"No, please, I don't want to go!"

"I know you don't think so. But you do. If you didn't, why are you letting me hold on to you like this?" Joseph nodded at his white knuckles clenched around Doru's shirt. "You're in charge here, Doru. You are almighty here. You can change this. But you won't."

They carried on, upward.

"No, you don't understand. I want you to let go, I'm commanding you, let me go!"

Joseph shook his head. "You don't. I know you don't, and you know it."

Fourth floor, and Doru maintained his resistance, pushing off from Joseph's body. To Joseph there was no real force behind Doru. He was simply laying his arms and hands carefully against Joseph's body, gently caressing him. But by the sounds and looks coming from Doru, he was doing everything in his power to come loose.

"Why don't you stop, Doru. Take a break. I'll let you have your peace before you're done." Fifth floor, and Joseph's words had calmed Doru a little. He still breathed heavily and cried, but he'd stopped the punching and kicking.

"Joseph, please, you don't have to do this."

"Yes, I do," Joseph said, rounding the corner of the stairs on the sixth floor.

"Why?"

"Why?" Joseph smiled. "You know why. Both you and Alyssa made claims that none of you were at the center of this. But you know what I realized?"

"What?" Doru sniffled.

"I'm at the center of this," Joseph said, pointing to his chest. "Of everyone in here, I'm the only one who's at the center of this. And I've realized my purpose here."

"No. It's not true. I'll give you another one. Like you said I'm almighty here!"

"Exactly, Doru."

Joseph dragged him up onto the seventh floor. They pushed through the door into the hallway and headed down toward Joseph's room.

"Who do you think gave me the purpose I have?" Joseph stopped to look at Doru for a second before they continued walking, a few more steps down to the hallway to Joseph's room.

"No, I promise, it's not true!"

"It is, Doru. Everyone in here is you. Baker and Carver is your company, your buddies. Bryan, Glenn, Clyde and Marcia. You put them in here to take care of you. You put Alyssa here to try and talk some sense into yourself, to force you out of here. And eventually . . . "

Joseph stopped outside 704, searching for the key in his pocket. He found nothing except for bent metal—the paper-clips. Doru had probably made the key disappear. Holding his palm out in front of himself, Joseph produced the key out of thin air.

"You put me here, the last resort, to take care of business when you couldn't yourself."

"It's not true, it's not true!"

"You know it is," Joseph said, swinging the door open. The room was empty, the lights were off. Joseph's suitcase was gone, the bed was made, and it looked like no one had ever been there.

"You're delaying the inevitable, Doru. Stop fighting me— stop fighting yourself."

"No," Doru barked, more angry than sad now, stepping up in front of Joseph, faces inches apart. "Please, don't," Doru begged. Joseph began walking back down the hallway toward the stairwell. "I'll do whatever you want, come on, you can be a god in here."

"You've been a god in here long enough, friend," Joseph whispered. "I got to do what I came here to do. You've begged me to do it since I arrived."

They stepped out into the hallway. The whirring and clanking noises from the elevator were louder than ever.

Joseph understood.

He walked over with Doru in tow and pressed the call button. The sound of the elevator traveling up filled the room.

"I'll just reappear again, like I did with you," Doru said. "All the times you tried those cuts on your arms. In the blink of an eye, we'll be sitting at lunch again."

"Sure, you will," Joseph winked. "Then how come you took the blades away from me? How come you made my suitcase disappear? You know I'll do it. You know I'll succeed."

"No, you won't. I'll make it go away."

"Sure," Joseph said carelessly. The elevator doors opened to a dark, freezing elevator shaft. The elevator wasn't there.

"These are for you, kid," Joseph said, handing Doru the paperclips from his pocket.

"What am I supposed to do with these?" Doru asked confused.

"No idea, but you'll need them." Joseph dropped them into his open palm and put his hand on Doru's shoulder, now holding onto both sides of him.

"You ready?"

The whirring and clanking of the elevator grew louder and louder, spinning and banging rapidly faster.

"I can't do it."

"I know you can't. That's why you put me in here to do it for you." Joseph's hands held Doru's shoulders firmly. His warm hands seem almost too big around the small shoulders. "I've been doing it so many times now, it's second nature to me."

"I don't want to be alone," Doru cried.

"You won't be," Joseph said, choking down a tear. "We'll go together."

With a brief glance at each other, Joseph swallowed and tipped them both into the elevator shaft.

"Open gate 704!" Joseph Podwall yelled. He saw the officer in the tower press the button and heard the familiar buzz as the cell doors slid open.

"I need a medic down here!" Joseph shouted into the radio on his chest. "It's 704 again. He's cut himself, properly this time! I need assistance."

The sirens went off, alarms blaring, notifying the prison of the emergency.

Joseph dropped down next to the prisoner. It had been many times already this month that the guy had tried to kill himself—more times than Joseph could remember—but it had never been as serious as it looked right now.

Blood pooled underneath the prisoner's lifeless body, the black-red circle expanding rapidly, sticking to the blue fabric on Joseph's knees. Other guards came rushing through, carrying blankets, grabbing the prisoner by the arms, yelling at him to stay awake. The last guard came carrying a stretcher, slamming it upright against the ceiling as he wiggled it through the cell door.

"One, two, three!" Joseph counted as the young guards combined their efforts to hoist the prisoner onto the stretcher.

It was not that he was heavy, more the opposite. He was fragile.

"Come on, come on, double time!"

The younger guards lifted with their knees and started

jogging as best they could toward the medical suite. Too fucking bad it was on the opposite side of the prison. More than once Joseph had suggested they ought to move such a troubled prisoner closer, but it had fallen on deaf ears. Having been sent to medical wings multiple times a month apparently didn't offer concern. Well, it was serious now.

Joseph looked around to see if he could figure out how the prisoner had done it. Last time it had been a poorly made shiv, crafted from a broken toothbrush. Once it had been a jagged edge on the bed frame. Not sharp enough to do any real damage—thankfully—but capable of drawing blood.

*What was it this time? Must have been something serious.*

Joseph turned in circles where he stood, unable to understand what weapon could have caused such tremendous damage. He checked in the toilet bowl, the sink, under the bed, and among the prisoner's personal items, but found nothing. Before leaving, he stood hovering over the pool, staring into it, transfixed, seeing if there could be anything hidden under the red. He took the bar of soap from the sink and carefully stirred it around, to see if the blood had disguised anything. *Nothing.* Standing back up, he left the cell in a sprint, happy to be leaving the screeching of the sirens.

JOSEPH BURST through the heavy double doors of the operating room. "How's he doing, Clyde?"

The medical doctor didn't reply, too occupied with trying to patch the prisoner's arm.

"Prepare a blood transfusion," he asked of his assistant, a young quiet woman who worked as the prison's only nurse. Joseph hadn't spoken to Marcia more than the one time.

"Clyde, talk to me," Joseph walked over to the opposing

side of the table the prisoner lay on. "Is he going to make it?"

"Put some on gloves and grab that tray over there." Clyde pointed to a silver tray with medical instruments on it.

"What? I don't have any medical training."

"Does it look like we have time to wait? Get me that tray!"

Joseph wasn't going to be asked thrice. He rolled up his sleeves and put on some gloves. He didn't know what most of the equipment on the tray was, but recognized a few scalpels and what looked like fishhooks—probably sewing needles. Joseph left the tray on top of the prisoner's chest—disrespectful, yes—but at least within easy reach for Dr. Clyde.

"Dammit, Joe! There's so much goddamn tissue damage. It's not looking good."

He never let any of the prisoners call him Joe, but he let it slide since it was the good doctor who was doing it—in a rushed panic, nonetheless.

"But he's going to pull through?"

"I don't know! Marcia? How are we coming along with that blood?"

"Coming, coming," she said.

"Joe, grab that stand behind you. Marcia, set an IV."

Joseph grabbed it and rolled it over next to Marcia, who stuck a needle into the prisoner's arm, right by the elbow.

"How do you know you've got the right type? Don't you need to do some tests?" Joseph asked, looking at the needle going into the prisoner's arm.

"He's been in here dozens of times already!" Clyde yelled at him.

*Of course.*

He took a step back to let the doctor and nurse work. They checked the prisoner's pulse, took his blood pressure—at least that's what Joseph assumed they were doing—and started administering the blood. Clyde was still dealing with the arm, closing the wound Joseph guessed, but it didn't look like he was successful.

"What the fuck is this?"

"What?"

"Get me that bowl over there." Clyde pointed to a deep silver dish, looking more like a bedpan than anything else.

Joseph brought it over and ended up holding it, not knowing where to put it.

Clyde grabbed a pair of small pliers off the tray sitting on the prisoner's chest and went digging into his arm with it.

"What is it?" Joseph asked again.

Clyde didn't answer, struggling with something in the patient's arm. Blood dripped off the table onto both Joseph's and Clyde's shoes, and though Joseph tried constantly to step out of it, Clyde didn't seem to even notice. Carefully he withdrew the pliers from inside the prisoner's forearms and dropped what he was holding into Joseph's silver bowl. It fell with a teeny clank, the blood oozing off it as it hit the metal.

"What is that?" Clyde asked with a muffled voice from behind his mask as Joseph raised the bowl to his face to have a closer look.

"Looks like . . . a piece of a paperclip? A broken-off piece of a paperclip," Joseph answered, turning back and looking at the arm. "You don't think?"

"Fucking hell," Clyde huffed, repositioning his headlamp and going back inside the arm.

"I couldn't find the weapon," Joseph began to explain. "Whatever he cut himself with, I couldn't find the instrument he used. I suppose this explains why. He cut himself with bits of paper clips—"

"And stuffed them inside his arm when he was done," Clyde finished. "Here's another one." He pulled the pliers out and dropped another piece of sharp metal into the bowl.

"Jesus Christ, he really went for the whole pincushion look, didn't he?" Clyde said. He looked in the middle of pulling another piece out, elbow aimed at the ceiling. Joseph heard a low gushing sound.

"Fuck!" Clyde yelled as blood spurted out on the floor.

"What happened?" Joseph stepped closer wanting to help, though not knowing how he could.

"A vein ruptured, fuck!" Clyde reached for instruments on the tray, yelling for Marcia to support him.

She ran to Clyde's side, pushing Joseph away as she handed the doctor instruments and clamps, obeying his every command.

In a haze, Joseph was left holding things, fetching things, and generally trying to stay out of the way. There was so much blood. *So much blood.* The amount that coated his knees and shoes was sticky if not completely dry already, and it weighed his clothes down as if they were soaking wet.

Moments went by, Clyde cursing under his breath until he chucked the pliers on the floor. He ripped off his gloves, his mask, and his cap, throwing it all on the floor. "He's gone."

Joseph stared at the body of the man he'd tried so many times to save. "What? You can't stop now, you have to try—"

"There's nothing I can do. I tried everything. Have a seat, Joe, you're looking pale."

"But, he's . . . you can just give him more blood, right?"

"He lost too much. That last paperclip made the hole even bigger. Couldn't put the blood back into him fast enough. Fucking idiot. I suppose that was his plan—sick and tired of me patching him up, so he put some booby traps in there for me. Fucking hell."

Clyde looked down at his mint green pants, soaked in dark blood. "Fucking worked though, didn't it?" Clyde laughed, the kind of morbid laugh only people who worked with these kinds of things had.

"I . . ." Joseph took a step closer, staring into the face of the prisoner. He looked like he could be alive, just sleeping. But the amount of blood loss was incredible. "So that's it then? He finally did it?"

"Yup," Clyde said, turning and walking over to the sink. Marcia nodded silently. "I'll start filling out the paperwork. You should go change, Joe. Then would you be a buddy and go tell the warden? Save me some time?"

Joseph hovered over the prisoner, staring at his peaceful face. "Sure, yeah, no problem," he muttered, looking down at his bloody shoes and knees.

*Dead, finally. After how many attempts?*

Every time, they'd manage to save him, and now, he was gone. Simple as that. It felt so trivial. Joseph was always the one to sound the alarm, the one to clasp the prisoner's wrist tight. Hell, one time he even carried him into medical over his shoulder.

He had helped Clyde resuscitate him once, breathing life back into him. All those times didn't mean anything anymore. It was over.

"I'll go do it right away," Joseph said, and left.

He stopped by his locker to change into clean jeans and shoes. Going back through the prisoner's wing, the aching of age and time burned in Joseph's bones. The adrenaline had flushed out of his system, he was no longer in fight or flight mode, and everything was heavy.

He walked up the stairs to the first hallway of cells and stopped for breath. Heading to the warden's office meant he'd have to go up another two flights and down the long, wide corridor to the north wing, but he remembered he had to pick up something first. An officer would come by later and hose down the prisoner's cell, removing any personal items and probably incinerate most of them. Joseph shuffled over; there was one thing he knew he had to save from that little six by eight-foot room.

Making sure he didn't step in more blood, Joseph danced around the middle of the floor and stopped in front of the sink where he picked up the faded and worn photograph, propped up behind the faucet. He grabbed it carefully and looked up at the white concrete wall above the sink, where a mirror usually would go. No mirrors for prisoners though, too easy to break and create a weapon out of.

"There we are. I'll make sure you're okay," he whispered.

"Joe?" A growling voice came from outside the cell. In the cell on the left, two meaty arms hung out through the bars, thick with black hairs.

"Hey, Baker," Joseph said.

Charles Baker, double life sentence for murder, yet probably the most peaceful prisoner they had in the joint.

"How's the kid doing this time?" Baker asked, his rough voice sounding like the bark of an aging dog. "He going to pull through?"

"Not this time, I'm afraid," Joseph said hesitantly, slapping the photograph lightly in the palm of his hand. A slender face appeared in the cell on the right, most of it hidden behind a scruffy, ginger beard.

"He gone?" George Carver asked. "Like for good?"

"For good, yeah. He bled out. Finally found the nerve to do it, after all those practice runs."

"A shame," Baker said, head hung low. "I kind of liked the kid. Really brightened up this place for old-timers like us, you know?"

"Yeah," Carver mused. "Damn kid could keep me up all night with his storytelling."

"Yeah, I'm . . ." Joseph wasn't sure what to say. His throat tightened. "I'm sorry about your loss, guys. I need to go tell the warden, just had to pick this up." He waved the photograph in front of them. "Don't want this to disappear now, do we?"

"Yeah, we're sorry too," Baker said. "Good thinking, Joe. Beautiful little girl, that one. See you around, yeah? Take it easy —you're looking older by the minute."

It was a long, silent trudge up to the warden's office. There was a heaviness over the prison, as if the prisoners were paying their respects, though most of them wouldn't have heard about what had happened yet.

"Morning, Bryan." Joseph nodded to the young guard as he stepped through to the waiting room at the end of the long hallway. It led off in three directions, including the one he'd come from. "Warden in?" he asked, pointing at the door right behind Bryan.

"Yeah, go right ahead. Bad morning, huh?" Bryan had undoubtedly heard the siren.

"You could say that." Joseph shrugged and knocked on the door.

"Come in," he heard from the other side, barely audible through the thick wood.

"Warden?"

"Yes, come in Joseph, what do you need?"

"It's about the prisoner in 704."

Joseph stepped through the doorway into the large office. It was in the oldest wing of the prison, in what was probably the oldest room in the wing. Anyone could tell it hadn't been renovated in a while. Red wallpaper with black floral patterns adorned the walls, making the room look small, and the wooden floor was grimy and dark from wear.

The only furniture was two wooden chairs in front of the large warden's desk, in the middle of which stood a golden plaque with the inscription: *Frank Mapp — Warden of Gatewell Correctional Facility.*

The warden was in his early sixties, a little older than Joseph, and had been in charge of The Gate for as long as he could remember.

"What about the prisoner in 704?" Frank grumbled.

"He's dead," Joseph said, walking in and positioning himself behind one of the empty chairs.

"What happened?" Frank asked, eying him over the top of his thick-rimmed glasses. He leaned back in his chair, making the fragile wood creak. Joseph squinted in fear of Frank's shirt buttons firing off across the room.

"Another suicide attempt, sir. Or well, not an attempt this time, I suppose."

"Christ." Frank exhaled, taking off his glasses, pinching the bridge of his nose. "Which one was he again?"

"Doru Amani," Joseph said. "Young guy, came in about two months ago, or so."

"The child killer?" Frank deadpanned.

"Yeah," Joseph said, lowering his head. "That's the one."

"Okay, fine. I'll notify the morgue. Do you need me to contact Glenn? Take care of the cell?"

"No that's fine. I'll sort it," Joseph said, turning to leave.

"Thank you, Joseph. It's good to have you out there on the floor."

"Sure thing, boss."

Joseph stepped out of the warden's office.

"Everything okay?" Bryan asked, a worried smile on the young boy's face.

"Nothing to worry about, Bryan. Just another day in prison. Is she in?" Joseph pointed to the third door, off to the side from the waiting room.

"As far as I know, yeah."

Joseph knocked on the door a few times, looking back at Bryan and faking a smile. He waited a little while before he knocked again.

"Come in!" he heard a soft voice yell.

Alyssa was on the phone when he entered, which was probably why she hadn't heard him the first time he knocked. She held up an elegant finger, indicating that she'd just be a moment.

Joseph took a seat in front of her desk.

Alyssa was the on-staff psychiatrist. She'd been sent out from the big city only half a year ago to whip the prison back into shape.

Joseph could tell from the smile on her face that she hadn't heard the sirens or any commotion. Alyssa held a finger up toward him again, *just a moment.* He nodded and forced a smiled. After another minute she said goodbye and hung up.

"What can I do for you, Joe?" she asked.

"It's Doru." Joseph cocked his head at her. He hadn't thought this far ahead. How would he break it, how could he begin to explain? In the end, his brain went with the obvious. "He's dead."

He saw the shift in her instantly—not sadness, not anger. Just disappointment and that familiar expectance, a sense of, *well there we have it, it finally happened.* She took her face in her hands, elbows on her desk, not meeting his gaze for a while.

"What happened?" she asked, but Joseph knew she knew what had happened.

"Suicide."

As one of the oldest guards, he and Alyssa had shared many a conversation about how to restructure the prison and how to take care of the prisoners. She'd been working with Doru for a while.

"Successful, this time. Cut his wrists open with a bunch of

paperclips it looks like. Stuffed them inside his arm like a little claymore for our doctor to find. Clyde didn't stand a chance when he tried removing them."

"Whoa." Alyssa removed her glasses, holding them in her hand as she stared out through the office. "I really thought we were making headway."

"Yeah, me too," Joseph said.

Alyssa cared for him, cared for all of them. She wanted them to thrive, to have activities to go to, to be heard. No one else in the prison had ever treated them like that before, treated them like people. Even Joseph—who thought he was a pretty good guy as far as prison guards went—hadn't thought of them like Alyssa.

"He was different. Every time we ended up here in my office after another episode, he'd go on about how he liked staying at The Gate. Talked about it as if it was a hotel. He said he admired you, how he'd like to be a prison guard when he was done serving his time, when . . . if he got out. Said he wanted to be brave like you, Joseph." She pinched the bridge of her nose. "He had his whole life in front of him. He wanted to have a job, shared all his dreams with everyone, talked about those two in the adjoining cells as his best friends."

"Baker and Carver," Joseph said. He wanted to say more, to mention how delusional Doru had to be if he believed he would ever get out, but decided to keep it to himself.

"And he missed his daughter so much, always bringing me that picture, showing me how happy she was."

"Yeah, she's a darling," Joseph said, remembering he'd brought the photograph. "I have it here actually." He held it up in front of his eyes with one hand, looking at the little girl one last time. "I figured enough things disappear from the cells as it is when people ship out. It'd be a shame if this got lost." He placed it on her desk, pushing it carefully toward her. "I figured maybe if the family wants any of his personal items, this might be one of them."

"Is there any family?" Alyssa picked up the photograph, studying it.

"I'm guessing parents at least, but . . ." Joseph swallowed. "His wife survived the attack, as far as I understood. I don't know the extent of her injuries, but if she didn't die in the hospital, I would assume she's on her feet and getting better by now." He pointed to the photograph in Alyssa's hands. "I was thinking maybe she'd like that?"

"Do you think so?" she asked, trying to disguise the frailty in her voice with a cough. "Wouldn't that bring back some dark memories?"

"Probably, but they could be worth it? I don't know. I'll let you decide that." He got up to leave. "Did they ever . . ." Joseph stopped to scratch his beard, one hand on the back of the chair. "Figure out why he did it? What the deal was?"

"We never got that far, unfortunately," Alyssa said, tipping her head to the side, leaning against her knuckles. "According to the police report, he attacked them both with a knife. His wife said there was no hesitation, but then again he—"

She stopped to look up at Joseph.

"He was completely different. As if he'd been somewhere else, not inside his own body. When we talked about it, he was full of remorse, so angry and sad at what had happened, but . . . but I don't know." She sighed. "He was kind of—"

"Kind of what?"

"No, it's stupid."

"No come on, tell me."

"He made up this . . . dream. This delusion. That he wasn't in a cell." She smiled at him. "You and I were there. A few other inmates. I'm not quite sure I understood." She looked away, smiling to herself. "I didn't indulge him, tried to get him back to the here and now. I kept focusing on trying to open up, asking about his childhood, his parents, the way his father treated him, to try and help him process. He always answered like he didn't see the problem, as if he hadn't tried to kill himself at all." Alyssa bowed her head. "I failed him."

"Hey now, you haven't failed anyone." Joseph took a step toward her desk. "You're the only one in here who's not content with leaving these people to rot. That counts for a lot. We did what we could with what we had. In the end it was Doru's choice."

Joseph sighed. "Make sure that picture gets to someone who wants it, okay?" he said, pointing to the picture of Doru and Melanie on her desk. "Or you know, keep it, I don't know. It was the only proper thing he owned. It'd be sad if it was thrown away."

"Yeah, I'll make sure," Alyssa said, picking it up with both hands.

"I'll head downstairs, leave you to your work."

Alyssa smiled in the corner of her mouth, but it quickly faded away.

"I'll take care of the cell, inform the other guards and the few prisoners who care."

"Thank you, Joseph." He turned to leave. Alyssa cleared her throat, which gave him pause. "How are you feeling? You knew him quite well after a while, didn't you?"

"I'm all right. I . . ." He rubbed a thumb and forefinger over his eyes and was surprised to find them wet. "I thought I could help him, you know. Be there for him, for all of them, to help them get through whatever struggles and burdens they carry. That's why I got into this line of work, after all. At least that's what I keep telling myself . . ."

He exhaled deeply and lowered his shoulders, feeling how

sore and tight his neck was. "But right now, it all feels a bit hopeless."

"You do more than you think, Joseph. But sometimes, even that is not enough. And that's not your fault. We'll just have to keep trying."

"Yeah, the world keeps spinning. I'll go take care of business downstairs now, feels like it's going to be a long day."

"All right then, Joseph. Talk to you later."

He popped out, but right before the door closed shut, he swung it half-way open and leaned back in. "Also, I've called the repair guys. They're coming by next week to look at the elevator."

If you find yourself in a situation where you feel unsafe or are feeling like you need some extra support, here are some mental health information and resources you may be able to utilize.

**United States**

- Mental Health Resources - http://www.healthline.com/health/mental-health-resources

- IPrevail - https://www.iprevail.com/

- Open Path Psychotherapy Collective - https://openpathcollective.org/

- 7cups - https://www.7cups.com/

- National Suicide Prevention Hotline - https://suicidepreventionlifeline.org/help-yourself/lgbtq/

- Trans LifeLine (US and Canada) - https://translifeline.org/

- The Trevor Project - https://www.thetrevorproject.
  org/get-help/#sm.0000c43c1912ptdxn
  rd3me2rtylex

## International & Outside US

- Global Suicide Hotline Resources - https://faq.
  whatsapp.com/general/security-and-privacy/
  global-suicide-hotline-resources/?lang=fi

- Find A Helpline - https://findahelpline.com/

- Stomp Out Bullying - https://www.
  stompoutbullying.org/international-suicide-
  prevention-resource

- SAVE - Suicide Awareness Voices of Education -
  https://save.org/find-help/international-resources/

- International Suicide Hotlines - http://www.
  suicide.org/hotlines/international-suicide-
  hotlines.html

- Depression and BiPolar Support Alliance - https://
  www.dbsalliance.org/crisis/suicide-hotline-
  helpline-information/

I've never been to prison, and I've never trapped my friends in an illusion. But the hotel is real, and my stay there is what sparked this story.

The real hotel is not an old, gothic building that creaks and moves in the wind. It's not even that old. As far as I can figure out, the hotel was bought by the corporate chain in 1989 (though the building itself is likely older). I was there for a conference sometime in the late summer of 2018. I didn't spend more than two nights, but I still vividly remember my time there.

The guy behind the reception desk was ever-present. When I arrived in the evening, when I came down for breakfast, when I returned from my conference that afternoon. He became Bryan, the receptionist at The Gate.

For a relatively modern hotel, it was very strange. The first thing was the hallway. It had matching carpet and wallpaper in a weird colorful pattern with lots of spots. It was psychedelic. I couldn't see where the wall ended and the floor began. The hallway to my room was crooked and bent in a way that seemed entirely unnecessary. Where I stepped out of the elevator, the hallway was perfectly straight, but as I walked toward my room, the hall curved like a snake with two steps randomly placed along the way.

The elevator worked, but it was very slow, seemingly

unstable. I always took the stairs going down, even if I was on the seventh floor.

The room is exactly as I describe it in the book: L-shaped with the bathroom immediately to your right, and then the bed further in around the bend. It was extremely small. I'm a pretty big guy, but luckily I'm not above average height so I lived. Also, I kept slamming the corner of the door into the ceiling. All the time.

Inside the room is where my story took life. I found the blood specks next to the mirror. Despite being clearly visible, I didn't see them until my second return to the room, which made me think someone could have been in there after I'd gone out. When I found bits of paperclips on the floor, I knew I had to write about this whole thing. It was the perfect backdrop for a story. Thus, I started working on At The Gate, which became the book you're reading now.

This book would never have seen the light of day without Maria's motivation and inspiration. If there's anyone I write for, it's you.

My good friend Ben has been invaluable help. I will always feel sorry for how many times I make you read my writing, but at least it seemed like you really liked this one. Your encouragement and helpful discussions are something I couldn't be without. I'll try to repay you some day, mate.

I also want to thank Cole, for always encouraging me and loving my stories.

And to my friend David, for reading and helping me rework an early draft of this book: thank you for being a mentor.

# About the Author

Trey Stone has studied archaeology in England, lived on an Arctic island for two years, and has more guitars than he has room for (the real problem is that his home is too small). He grew up on a farm in rural, western Norway, and has a bunch of siblings, half-siblings and in-laws, and is uncle to—oh, I don't know—twenty or so kids. They're all pretty awesome, he thinks. It's difficult to remember who's who anymore.

Trey as been telling stories for as long as he can remember. He used to create "books" when he was little by folding and stapling a bunch of paper together to write and draw scenes on the pages. He wrote a bunch of short stories when he was younger and tried his hand at a fantasy novel as a teen (but hardly any of that got anywhere)—then he finally wrote his first thriller five years ago and just never stopped. Thankfully!

Trey Stone is also the author of *A State of Despair* and *The Consequence of Loyalty*. You can find Trey on Amazon, Goodreads, and Twitter, or on his website.

**Website**

https://trey-stone.com/